Praise for Beth Williamson

"...brings fans another story of the older generation of the remarkable Malloy family, with a beautifully realized setting and a number of charming historic details."
—RT Book Reviews on *The Fortune*

"Another great western from Beth Williamson. I loved it and look forward to more."
—Mrs. Condit & Friends Read Books on *The Fortune*

"...a creative, heartwarming and sizzling journey of high adventure and new beginnings."
—RT Book Reviews on *The Prospect*

"...a sexy adventure and beautiful love story."
—Romance Junkies on *The Prospect*

"...one of my favorite books yet. This story just grabbed a hold of me and wouldn't let go."
—Book Obsessed Chicks on *The Jewel*

"*The Jewel* was by far the most intense of these last three stories in this series but it was also my favorite."
—Guilty Pleasures Book Reviews

Look for these titles by Beth Williamson

Now Available:

The Gem

Beth Williamson

SAMHAIN
PUBLISHING

Samhain Publishing, Ltd.
11821 Mason Montgomery Road, 4B
Cincinnati, OH 45249
www.samhainpublishing.com

The Gem
Copyright © 2015 by Beth Williamson
Print ISBN: 978-1-61923-035-4
Digital ISBN: 978-1-61922-867-2

Editing by Amy Sherwood
Cover by Kim Killion

First Samhain Publishing, Ltd. electronic publication: July 2015
First Samhain Publishing, Ltd. print publication: July 2015

Dedication

To those men and women who see beneath the prickly exterior some of us show to the world, to find the beautiful soul who lives beneath. Love transforms us into the beautiful creatures our mates see. True love isn't blind, it does not see what's on the outside, but only the heart that beats beneath.

Chapter One

Fort Laramie, Wyoming Territory
May 1858

The surefire way to goad Charlie Chastain into doing something was to forbid her from doing it.

While her two older nephews were out with their father, Mason, and the youngest was napping, Isabelle cornered Charlie. Lured by the promise of fresh cookies, she'd arrived only to find a dress lying on the chair, waiting to attach itself to Charlie's form. Like a blue snake.

Iz blocked the door, her chin at a stubborn tilt. "I forbid you to leave this house." Isabelle, the most beautiful of the four Chastain sisters, had striking green eyes and light brown hair. Even after three children, she was stunning to look at. Charlie, on the other hand, had frizzy, kinky hair with every shade of brown and red, and boring hazel eyes. She wasn't tall or short, she was round in all the female places, but she was also muscular. Not many women were built like her, nor did they do the amount of physical labor she performed daily. Charlie knew she wasn't attractive and it didn't bother her a bit.

"You know I could knock you out of the way and leave." Charlie folded her arms, her temper burbling like a pot on an open fire.

"I just want you to try on the dress. That's all. See how it fits." Isabelle's expression was tight with a forced smile.

"No, hell no." Charlie glared at Iz. "You tricked me."

"I didn't trick you." Her sister's cheeks reddened with guilt. "I made cookies, but I wanted to show you this lovely dress I had made for you." She gestured to the garment. "The ladies would like to get to know you better."

Charlie wasn't going to believe that for a minute. "No they don't. I'm an oddity. A girl that doesn't act like one. They want to make me into one of them and—" She shuddered. "Marry me off to one of the single men."

The senior officers at the fort were married, with their wives holding court. The junior officers were mostly unmarried. Not one of them interested her. Hell, no man had ever interested her. Charlie had stopped wondering if she'd ever find that kind of love—the answer was no. Her world was small, the way she liked it. If only she didn't wonder about what life would be like if she did have a man in her life other than Eli. He didn't count, since he was her best friend.

Charlie didn't understand why Isabelle couldn't just let her be.

"I want to see you happy." Iz frowned. "Spending all your time up to your elbows in blood can't be what you want to do for the rest of your life. You should marry Eli."

"How do you know?" Charlie's ire grew with every passing moment. "You have your perfect life with your perfect husband and perfect children. You don't know a damn thing about me. I can't marry Eli. He's my best friend, not someone who could be my husband."

To be truthful, Charlie was to blame for shutting her sisters out. She didn't want them to know every detail of her life—or sometimes, *any* details.

Charlie was as wild and untamed as the Wyoming wilderness. She refused to be forced into being the ideal of what the societal rules said she should be. It began on the trip west from New York, when she discovered rough men and their rougher ways. The men who led the wagon train were fascinating and appealing. Charlie had immediately felt a kinship with them.

Then everything had gone to hell and she'd become an orphan, set adrift in the world with only her sisters to ground her. Charlie had fought against the sadness and despair that threatened, the darkness that crept around inside the deepest recesses of her heart. Instead, she found what she could do well.

Hunt.

She didn't expect it. Not for a girl who spent the first fifteen years of her life in New York. She'd not even seen an elk or bison or bear until she went west with her family. Now that she lived in the Wyoming Territory, those animals and more had become a common sight. Who knew the Chastain sisters would be such crack shots? None of them had held a pistol or rifle until their father made sure they knew how to use one. Western women were as tough as the men. They had to be or they didn't survive.

Charlie took to hunting like a duck to water. Within a year she had surpassed Isabelle and then everyone else at the fort. She didn't want to be schooled or sit around doing feminine chores. So she took her skills and put them to good use—hunting, dressing, skinning and selling her catch and the wares made from it.

Now she was one of the most sought-after hunters, taking on one crazy job after another. She had autonomy to do what she wanted, when she wanted. After Eli had helped her build a cabin at the corner of her sister's house along with a shed for smoking meat, she had her own home, albeit connected to Isabelle's.

She tried to resist, damn how she tried, but it never failed to chap her ass to be told what to do or not to do. Her older sister Isabelle thought it was her duty to keep Charlie in check and civilized. Isabelle had taught her sister all the niceties ladies needed to know. Sometimes Charlie followed them, but more often she didn't. Trying to be a lady was a slippery slope she had no desire to navigate, but she tried for Isabelle's sake. She loved her sister and didn't want to be a disappointment.

But there were just some things Charlie couldn't do.

Was there no escape?

Isabelle's expression turned to one of sadness. "I'm not trying to change you. I thought if you attended this tea with the officers' wives, you could make some new friends. Perhaps try something different. I just want you to be happy."

Charlie snatched a cookie from the plate on the table. "I *am* happy." With that lie crowding her throat, she turned to leave her sister's house.

"Please stay. At least until people are due to arrive." Isabelle sat on the settee and patted the cushion. "Please."

Charlie crammed the cookie into her mouth and sat down with little grace. She wore trousers, so she sat with her knees open, waiting for Isabelle to scold her.

"Your tactics aren't working." Isabelle raised one brow. "I know you're a grown woman, but acting like a spoiled child is not the answer to anything."

"I'm not," Charlie lied to herself and her sister. It seemed today was the day she couldn't quite tell the truth.

Charlie had everything she needed. Yet nothing she wanted.

"Did you talk to Eli about your plan?" Isabelle nibbled at a cookie.

Charlie's heart dropped. "No, and I won't. It's none of his business."

Charlie had a grand scheme in which she planned to leave the fort for good. Nothing was keeping her there except Isabelle and her children. Charlie felt stifled, trapped in a world she never asked for. She was going to set off on her own by the end of the summer. Her mind was made up.

Isabelle shook her head. "I sincerely doubt that. I've never seen you so, um, flustered. By anything or anyone. Not since—"

"Stop, I don't want to talk about this." Charlie glared, refusing to go down the dark path she had hidden from everyone.

"Just because you don't want to talk about it doesn't mean there's nothing to discuss. You've never lived alone or on your own." Isabelle took her hand. "You never shared what Cam—"

Charlie jumped to her feet, knocking the table over. Cookies, plates and everything Isabelle had set flew across the room. "Shut up, Iz. Just shut up!"

Without another word, she yanked the door open. Her youngest nephew Samuel stood in the bedroom doorway to her right, his hair in a cloud around his head, thumb in his mouth, his eyes wide. She hadn't meant to scare him, but she couldn't sit and listen to Isabelle any longer.

Charlie couldn't be the normal female her sisters wanted her to be. She was abnormal, and that was how she would remain. No matter what happened, she could not change the past, and it shaped her future, crooked as it was.

She had to do something to stop her sister and the women of the fort from marrying her off. Living on her own would do that quite nicely. Now she had to figure out what she would do to survive on her own. She would start by avoiding dresses. Forever.

"Shitshitshitshit!" Eli dropped his hammer into the dirt and shook his hand. Pain radiated up his thumb and arm until even his damn jaw hurt. He'd been distracted by his thoughts, which made him fodder for anyone who was nearby.

"Fixit, you need a real man to show you how to use that thing?" The taunt came from the bunkhouse, a mere ten yards from where he worked on the fence. Worse, he recognized the voice. Sergeant Volner stepped into the sunshine, his bearded face twisted into his usual sneer.

Eli picked up the hammer and squeezed until he felt sick from the pain. That was real, not the stupidity of a soldier like Volner.

"Guess you can grip it, but can you use it?" Volner snorted at his own witticism. Idiot.

Eli had discovered years ago if he ignored the bullies, they lost interest in bothering him. They still called him Fixit, but he likely would never lose that particular moniker. Back when he was a fifteen-year-old boy, he hadn't known any better. Skinny, clumsy and worse, a stutterer, he lost his temper a thousand times at the name Fixit. It took years before he could hear it without flinching. Regardless of how smart he was, people still saw him as that awkward boy.

Volner took great pleasure in causing others discomfort. Eli wasn't a skinny, gangly boy anymore, but that didn't stop fools from picking on him. Eli was also as tall, if not taller, than the sergeant, but Volner carried a weapon and that gave him false courage.

Most days Eli could ignore Volner and his underling Corporal Oxley, but it had been a shitty day. Volner was like a giant vulture, picking at a wounded animal, willing it to die so he could feast. He stood at just over six feet, with wide shoulders and a narrow waist, greasy brown hair and nearly colorless blue eyes. His nose was hooked and his chin pointed, lending more credence to his carrion-eating visage.

Oxley was the opposite, short, round, with wispy blond hair and chocolate-brown eyes that were lost in his chubby cheeks. He followed Volner around like a pet, performing any and all tasks without question, no matter how distasteful to anyone else. Eli had even seen Oxley eat a dead rat raw because Volner told him to. While the sergeant was stupid and annoying, Oxley was more dangerous because he had no inhibitions.

Eli stayed out of their way as much as possible. He had no desire to run afoul of either of them, but today was different. His temper was riled.

"Don't you have work to do? The government pays you to be a soldier, not a donkey dick." Eli turned his back and picked up another nail.

The attack, when it came, was expected. Eli needed it. Almost craved it. He ducked as the beefy arm swung. He countered with a hammer swing to the knee. Volner dropped like a stone, squealing and moaning. Oxley jumped on Eli's back, his sharp wrist digging into Eli's neck.

Eli swung his upper body forward, throwing the corporal into the dirt with a solid thump. He bared his teeth at Oxley.

"I got work to do. You two stop fussing with me or I'll tell the captain what you do out behind the trading post." Eli was invisible much of the time, and people forgot he was around, watching and observing. The soldiers were a mixed lot, some good, some bad, some downright rotten like Oxley and Volner.

"Fixit, you broke my fucking knee!" Volner clutched his leg and shot daggers with his eyes at Eli.

"Nah, it's just bruised. You'll live, but you'll limp." Eli rubbed his neck and glared at Oxley as the man got to his feet and scrambled away. "Keep your distance. I ain't gonna play no more with you."

Eli picked up his hammer from the dirt a second time and waited. Volner growled and lumbered to his feet.

"Dirty fighting, Fixit."

Eli shrugged. "I give what I get." It wasn't the first time, nor would it be the last time, the two soldiers bothered him. Since the soldiers had arrived at the fort, they'd taken it upon themselves to pick a fight with him, trip him, throw food at him; before them, it had been trappers. Eli had endured it for years, but the difference was that now he could fight back. He no longer swallowed his pride or accepted the abuse. Volner and Oxley would learn to leave him be. Eventually.

"What's going on here?" Captain Hamilton, the current commander of the fort, stepped up with a scowl on his face. He'd only been at Fort Laramie for a mere month and hadn't taken full command of the soldiers. He was the same type of officer that had come west previously, full of big ideas and the urge to tame the wild country. He hadn't yet discovered there wasn't a man alive who could tame the territory.

"A misunderstanding, captain." Eli stared at Volner, daring him to contradict him.

"Yep, ain't nothin'." Volner limped away, his gaze promising retribution. Oxley was right behind him.

Some days Eli wished the soldiers would disappear and not come back. That would leave the fort vulnerable to Indian attack. Even so, it was a tempting wish.

"Mr. Sylvester, when you're done with this fence, there are repairs required in the officers' mess." The captain was a tall, narrow-faced man whose red mustache was wider than his cheeks. He had kind blue eyes, which would not serve him well at the fort. The soldiers he commanded were a mixture of men who were hiding from a crime, their past or their future. It did not bode well for an idealistic officer like Hamilton.

"Yes, sir." Eli returned to his work and waited for the captain to move on.

He didn't.

"Mr. Sylvester, I have a question for you." The captain twisted his mustache between his fingers and his gaze skittered around rather than meet Eli's.

Eli paused, his hammer above the nail. "I got work to do, sir."

"Oh, yes, I know that. I have a question about someone you know. Her name is Charlotte Chastain." Hamilton cleared his throat and resumed twiddling with his facial hair.

The mention of Charlie's name made Eli's hackles stand up. His best friend was an unusual sort of female. She didn't fit into anyone's mold and she also cursed more than any man Eli had ever known.

He also loved her with every particle of his being, and she didn't know it.

"I know Charlie." Eli kept his response vague, wondering what the captain wanted.

"It's been suggested to me that Charlotte would be a likely candidate for a wife. I was to meet her today at her sister Mrs. Bennett's house, but she was unavailable." Hamilton finally met Eli's gaze. "I would ask you to introduce us properly if you can."

Eli wanted to punch him, cause enough damage to the man's handsome face that Charlie could hardly bear to look at him. Jealousy roared through Eli on a red wave. He swallowed it back although it tasted of sawdust and ashes.

"I would think that is Isabelle's job. I ain't the right person to ask." Eli slammed the nail in place followed by another, then another.

Captain Hamilton still stayed put. What was the man doing? Eli wasn't about to give Charlie to him as though she were a commodity to be picked up at the mercantile. No one owned her or her future. Eli hazarded a guess that Charlie had deliberately avoided meeting the captain. She didn't want to be ordered about by anyone, least of all a blue coat.

"I don't disagree with you, Mr. Sylvester. If you have the opportunity, I would appreciate an introduction." The man shuffled his feet in the dirt and Eli almost bit through the nail he had in his teeth. "Such as now."

Eli's gaze snapped to the left and he spotted Charlie walking toward them. His gut tightened at the sight. He would do anything for her, no matter how big or small. But he would not give her to this soldier.

Damn woman had shit timing. He turned back to his work, refusing to look at her. Eli had trouble resisting her and she damn well knew it.

"Eli, don't pretend you didn't see me." Charlie put her foot up on the railing of the fence, her boot caked with mud.

"I'm busy." Eli tried to forget the captain stood there, but Charlie was no shrinking violet. There wasn't a thought in her head she didn't allow to escape from her mouth.

"You the new captain?"

Eli glanced up to see her peering at Hamilton as though he were being interviewed for the job he already had.

"Yes, ma'am." The captain speared Eli with a glare.

"Charlie, this is Captain Hamilton." A little devil took hold of his tongue. "Captain, this is Miss Charlotte Marie Chastain."

Her eyes narrowed and her mouth tightened. She hated being called by her full name almost as much as she hated wearing dresses.

"Charlie. Just Charlie. Eli must've had a knock to his goddamn head." She curled her lip at Eli. "What the hell has gotten into you?"

The captain's eyes widened, no doubt at the amount of cussing coming from a female's mouth. "It's a pleasure to meet you, Miss Chastain."

Charlie didn't bother to acknowledge the captain's polite words. She must've been on a tear and Eli contributed to her bad mood with no regret.

"Try to remember you have manners. The captain is new to the fort and is meeting everyone who lives here." Eli watched her expression harden, but he couldn't stop himself from chastising her. His day had now gone from bad to worse.

"Captain." She touched the brim of her hat. "Eli, I was gonna ask you about hunting, but now I won't. You're a jackass." Charlie stomped away, the outline of her hips and ass clear in the deerskin trousers she wore. Her generous curves haunted his dreams.

"I, uh, that was unexpected." Captain Hamilton took off his hat and wiped his brow with a snowy white handkerchief.

"She's never going to be anything but." Eli gestured with the hammer at her retreating back. "Charlie does whatever she pleases, consequences be damned."

"I can see that. She also has, ah, a colorful vocabulary."

Eli shrugged. "Picked that up on the wagon train heading west."

"She was a pioneer. That takes strength and fortitude." The other man appeared more interested. Damn it.

"Her family left New York for the Oregon territory. Two of her sisters settled southwest of here. Her parents died and she and her sister Isabelle came to the fort to live. They've been here more than ten years now." Eli didn't want to tell tales about Charlie, but none of what he said was a secret. Anything else Charlie had confided in him wouldn't be shared.

"I met Mrs. Bennett and her husband. He is quite a teacher, and I hear she has kept people at the fort hale and hearty." The captain nodded to himself. "Good civilians are hard to come by in a military fort."

"It wasn't always military." Eli didn't want to continue the conversation, but the man had to be told the truth. "It was a trading post, started by trappers. The military came in recent and took over."

Hamilton straightened his shoulders. "The military needs to take control in situations where our citizens are in peril. The Indians are hostile, Mr. Sylvester. We're protecting our sovereign rights."

The entire situation left a bad taste in Eli's mouth. He was done talking. "I got work to do, captain."

"Oh yes, yes, of course. Thank you for introducing me to Miss Chastain. It's most appreciated." Hamilton put his hat on and strode away, his blue uniform shining brighter than a peacock in the sun.

Eli was finally alone with his work. He was not, however, at peace. His thoughts returned to Charlie and to what awaited him at the end of his chores. A lonely Saturday night.

Charlie was annoyed. At everyone. At everything. After Iz tried to force her to wear a dress, drink tea and make nice with some ladies, nothing had gone right. Her day had been ruined. To make matters worse, she saw Gunther Becker unloading a wagon at the general store. The big man reminded her of all she tried to forget from ten years earlier. She resented him for staying at the fort even if he hadn't spoken to her since his arrival. Guilty or innocent of any crimes, he was a walking nightmare from which she couldn't escape.

She stomped all the way back to her cabin, then slammed the door for good measure, which Isabelle no doubt heard. It didn't help her mood at all. Charlie had acted stupid and childish, and now she was mad. It was foolish, but sometimes she couldn't help herself. She sat down hard in the chair Eli had made and crossed her arms.

Life used to be simple. She was not the same person she had been when she lived in New York. That girl had died somewhere on a snowy landscape in the Wyoming Territory. Dark memories bubbled up into her throat and she swallowed them back before they were allowed to escape.

In her mind she knew Isabelle was only trying to help her, but her temper seemed to have control over her. Charlie had taken pains to hide the worst of her anger. Occasionally it took hold of her like a fist, clenching so hard she struck out at the nearest target. Today, it was Iz, Eli and anyone else who'd crossed her path.

She blew out a breath, and just like that, her fury was gone. Charlie ran her hands down her face. She would have to behave herself and stop being rude to others. Her cussing had been bad for years, and she had stopped it most of the time. Her temper and her cursing were tied together like evil twins.

One of her secrets, something she didn't share with most people, was that she loved to bake. She didn't always have what she needed, but when she did, the act of making something delicious like bread or biscuits or the most heavenly treat, a cake, was pleasurable. She had sneaked a few cups of flour from Iz and she could make something. Perhaps it would help make her peace with things.

Charlie needed get back to the work she had to do, but she could finish it later. Cleaning a weapon could always wait a few hours. Decided, she stoked the fire in the stove in the corner and got to work baking. The feel of the dough between her fingers soothed her. The act of making something from a bunch of other ingredients fascinated her. She wasn't a good cook, but she didn't starve. Baking, however, she had a natural affinity for.

Over the last ten years, Charlie had taken great pains to keep her distance from most people. It wasn't that she didn't like them. She didn't trust them. Very few folks were in her life and she liked it that way. Her sisters, their husbands and children, and Eli. No one else.

The thought of spending time with a man, a complete stranger, made her physically uncomfortable. She had no desire to get married or have children. She left that particular task to her three sisters. Francesca already had five sons, Josephine had two sons and Isabelle had somehow birthed three. So many boys! Strange for a family of four females.

If Charlie had a need to cuddle a child, she had ten nephews to choose from. No, she did not want to be a mother and spend all her time terrified something would happen to her child. The world was a dark place and danger lurked in all corners. Charlie was an expert at every weapon she picked up—no one could or would hurt her if she could stop them.

She liked her solitude and her independence. Her cabin, and her skills as a hunter, tanning hides and creating tools from bone, along with her loud mouth, generally kept people at a distance socially. Perhaps she'd built a wall, but it was hers to build and live behind.

While the biscuits baked, she worked on sharpening some bone into utensils. The soldiers in the fort didn't much care for them. Her buyers were the women who worked in the mess hall, the soldier's wives and the locals. She made a good living selling her wares, most times by request, but using the bones from the animals gave her extra income. Charlie didn't need a man.

She pulled a pan of fluffy biscuits from the stove, their delicious aroma decorating the air. She sucked in the buttery scent and smiled. Who would have thought she would enjoy such a feminine activity? If she had her way, no one would ever know. Except Iz. And Eli. He wouldn't tell, or she'd punch him senseless. Such was her relationship with Eli. She would bring half the biscuits to him. It was a thing friends did for each other.

She looked around the house, but she didn't have a basket to put the biscuits in. She had racks of antlers, a pile of skins, a barrel of jerky and not much else besides her few clothes and weapons. Normally she would eat what she baked, but she needed to bring these to Eli. She wouldn't ask Isabelle because then Charlie would have to apologize and she wasn't ready for that yet.

She puzzled over what to do since she also didn't want people to see her with fresh-baked biscuits. They might start believing she was a regular female, and she couldn't let that happen. Her leaving the fort depended on people accepting she was as capable as a man. Female skills weren't important to "the plan".

She took two small antlers and wove them together into a bowl-like shape, then put a clean rag around them, securing the cloth in a knot. It wasn't perfect, but it would work. She placed half a dozen piping hot biscuits in the makeshift bowl, then looped the rag around the top to secure it closed.

Eli didn't expect a treat and it was her way of apologizing for all the times she'd snapped at him. She took advantage of his friendship so often, she was surprised he remained her friend.

Elijah Sylvester was a unique man. He didn't fit in with what people expected and that made him different. Charlie had known him from the day she'd arrived at the fort. They'd grown up side by side like a brother and sister. Two odd individuals amongst the rest of the population. It was no wonder they were drawn to each other. Eli was the one and only friend she had.

That thought stopped her as she stepped out of her little cabin. She had separated herself from everyone and everything purposefully. Charlie didn't like to be around people and she took great pains to avoid them. No one understood that better than Eli. He wasn't much for talking, but he was damn good at just being there, no matter what.

So what if she had only one friend? She didn't want a dozen friends if they weren't worth more than spit in the wind. Most people only did for themselves and not for others. Some had good hearts and did good deeds, but they were the exception. Charlie didn't put herself into a position to find out if people were the good kind or the bad kind.

After putting her pistol on her hip, one knife in her boot and the other in the sheath on her back, she picked up the makeshift bowl and left. Charlie was never unarmed. Ever.

The fort was bustling with activity in the late afternoon. The air rang with the sound of a blacksmith's hammer, horses whinnying, shouting and grunting from soldiers digging a hole, clucks of chickens in the coop and a few dogs barking. Normal life in the fort, but Charlie, she watched it all. She didn't participate in any of the activities. Some people nodded at her as she passed. Others flat out ignored her. She didn't take offense. When they needed her services, they would come see her.

With summer coming on, game would be plentiful and she would be busy for months. Today she would take some time to be with Eli and get out some frustration by hunting. He might need to do that as well, given how hard he worked every day at keeping the fort in shape while the soldiers rode him harder than the horses.

She walked around the side of the mercantile to the shed behind the building where Eli lived. The door was closed, but she knocked and walked in, her biscuits in hand, which fell to the floor when she was rendered speechless.

Eli was naked.

Chapter Two

Everything changed the moment she saw Elijah Sylvester naked.

Charlie should have knocked on the door again. She should have shouted to him before she entered his cabin. But she hadn't. He was her best friend. They had spent time together every day for the last ten years. She couldn't imagine what her life would be like without Eli at her side. As her friend, not as a man.

But now she'd ruined that friendship because of her impetuous actions—she walked in to find Eli naked, covered in soap. Although it was merely seconds, she lived a lifetime as she drank in the sight of the man she never knew beneath his ill-fitting clothes.

Soap bubbles clung to his body, accentuating golden muscles and sinew. Eli was tall and lean, but his form was built of elegant lines. How had he hid this from her for ten years? She'd never thought of him as a man, and now she would never think of anything else.

He ruined everything by revealing himself. Never mind that it was her fault or that he seemed as mortified as she was. He held a bucket over his head, presumably to rinse himself into the hip bath he stood in. His arms shook, as the water must've weighed a good bit.

He dumped the water over his head. The bucket clattered to the floor and he wiped the suds from his face. As he reached for the towel on the back of his chair, she moved closer to him, without thought. He jumped back and slipped on the wet floor, landing on his ass with a howl of pain, probably obtaining a few splinters in the process.

"Shit, Eli!" Charlie was right there beside him, inches away from his naked body.

Her heart stuttered and her thoughts scattered. She couldn't look away.

"What are you doing here?" His voice was rough as sandpaper.

"I came to see if you wanted to go hunting tomorrow. I saw Big Buck." She held out her hand. "And you're naked." She sounded like the village idiot. Her cheeks were hotter than a forge, burning up her face.

He scrambled backwards and got to his feet. She was painfully aware of how close she was to him. Close enough she could smell him, touch him—hell, she could kiss him.

Holy shit. What was wrong with her?

"I know I'm naked." He snatched the towel off the chair, the end slapping her in the leg. She winced and made a face. She couldn't decide to laugh or cry as he wrapped the towel around his torso. Unfortunately the thin fabric did not hide the body she'd seen in its full glory. "Why didn't you wait until I invited you in?"

She shook her head. "I didn't know you'd be naked."

"Oh, for God's sake, Charlie, would you forget about me being naked?" He tightened the towel with a jerk.

"I can't." She stepped closer, her curiosity overcoming the ridiculous reaction she couldn't control. "You're not what I expected."

"You need to leave." He pointed at the door.

She reached up and ran her hand down his shoulder to his arm. "I didn't know you had these under your shirt." Her fingers traced the curve of a muscle. "Hell, I saw Mason without his clothes, but he didn't have these. You hide yourself from people. It's no wonder. The women would chase you if they knew what was under your clothes." She touched the other shoulder and his small nipples pebbled to a point. Men's nipples did that too?

"Jesus, Charlie. What are you doing? What are you saying?" He stepped back to put at least a foot between them. Her hand traveled with him, the heat from his skin almost burning her.

Her gaze snapped to his and her hand finally dropped to her side. "I don't know."

The moment stretched between them, the air crackling. Charlie managed to suck in a breath, but her chest was heavy. It was like breathing underwater.

"I'm sorry, Eli." She shook her head. "I saw Big Buck and we've been chasing him for a couple years now. That damn elk is slippery and I wanted to tell you... And then I made biscuits." She glanced at the floor, embarrassment roaring through her. "Shit. I'm sorry." The last two minutes were the strangest of her life.

His eyes narrowed. "Wait, did you just apologize?"

She scowled at him. "Don't act like I don't apologize."

He snorted. "It ain't a word you know."

"I don't do it often, but I do apologize." Of course she was lying. Both of them knew it. "I didn't mean to barge in on you. It wasn't nice."

"You're never nice."

She huffed a frustrated breath—he was right, of course. "Yes I am." She fibbed again. "And I'm, uh, sorry about seeing you naked."

"I reckon you got an eyeful you didn't expect." He stared at the floor, avoiding direct eye contact.

"I did. Um, do you want to go hunting?" He had gone with her many times over the years. Eli was a true friend, even if he was rough around the edges.

"Maybe." He shrugged, although he looked like he wanted to run screaming from the cabin.

"I, uh, should let you get some clothes on so you can do whatever you were gonna do." As she turned toward the door, she tasted disappointment on her tongue, bitter and unwelcome. "If you want to go hunting, meet me at the edge of the woods tomorrow at six." Then she tossed the makeshift basket on the table and glanced back, sweeping his body with her scrutiny.

Shit.

The cool air had hit his wet skin moments before Eli had realized he wasn't alone. He had stopped, frozen in place, while Charlie had stood in the doorway, her mouth open. Then of course, he'd fallen on his ass, which was not an unusual occurrence, but he generally wasn't naked in front of her. He'd never been naked in front of her.

After working hard all day, he'd been hotter than hell, sweat-soaked and exhausted. While he should have gone and bathed in the river, the current was running strong and he didn't feel like fighting it. He'd decided to wash with a bucket of cool water instead.

The last thing he expected was for Charlie to bust through the door. She'd looked as surprised as he was. His body had reacted to her nearness and his nakedness. Damned if his dick hadn't hardened almost instantly. Her gaze had dropped and his balls tightened.

Somehow she hadn't run screaming from the cabin, but *he'd* wanted to. Hell, he'd wanted a hole to open up in the floor and swallow him. She had only been there for two minutes, but it'd felt like a lifetime. Now that she'd gone, he sat down hard in the chair and put his head in his hands.

He'd loved her for so long, from the moment he'd seen her if he were honest with himself. At fifteen, she'd been a foul-mouthed, crazy-haired girl and he'd been enchanted instantly. Now, ten years later, she'd found him naked and the only thing that had been between them was a threadbare towel.

It had either been a dream come true or a nightmare.

He had wanted to kiss her, taste her, worship her body as though she were a goddess in human form.

Damn. Eli had never been so turned around in his life.

If there wasn't the possibility of her walking back through the door, he would wrap his hands around his cock and relieve the pressure, the ache, the goddamn longing built up inside him. Other than some fumbling with a few whores and one soldier's widow, Eli had little experience with women. Perhaps what he needed was to forget his dreams of marrying the woman he loved and find a wife.

No more moping because he loved a woman who thought of him as her best friend on a good day, her assistant most others. Hell, he had no excuse for not looking for a woman who would marry him, regardless of how scarce females were in the territory. Charlie never would be his wife, no matter what had just happened. Eli needed to move on. Ten years was too long to moon over a woman. It was past time he started living his own life.

He would find a good woman to marry him and put Charlie behind him.

After leaving Eli's cabin, Charlie walked as fast as her legs could take her toward Isabelle. Soon she gave up all decorum and ran. She didn't care if people stared at her or what they thought. She needed to talk to her sister. Now.

While she would normally walk through the door, Charlie burst in, breathless and almost vibrating with confusion. Isabelle was setting the table. Her welcoming smile faded as she took in Charlie's expression.

"I thought you came for supper. You didn't, did you?" Isabelle set the plates on the table. "What's wrong?"

Charlie heaved air in and out like a bellows, trying to stop the panic that threatened to overwhelm her. "I need help, Iz. I saw Eli naked."

Isabelle blinked and hesitated. "Supper will be ready in fifteen minutes. Let's sit and talk in my room."

Charlie let out a sigh and followed her sister. Dismayed to realize her hands were shaking, Charlie sat down heavily on the chest at the end of the bed.

Isabelle poured water into a basin then soaked a cloth and wrung it out. She sat down on the chest and started wiping Charlie's face. The moment reminded Charlie so much of her mother that tears sprang to her eyes.

"I wish Maman was here." Charlie spoke before she could stop the words.

Isabelle nodded. "Sometimes I do too. When I held Andrew for the first time, I wanted her there so much I wept. She should have lived to see her grandchildren. But then I remember both Maman and Papa are with us."

Charlie let her sister wash her face. The cool water refreshed her overheated skin. "What do you mean, they're with us?"

"I don't know what is beyond this life, but I believe our parents are keeping watch over all four of us." Isabelle wrung the cloth out again.

"How is that possible?" Charlie was more than skeptical.

"Whatever awaits us after death, I feel them with me. When I held Andrew, I swear I smelled Maman's rosewater soap. Whether they can be beside us, they are with us when we triumph, when we celebrate and when we despair." Isabelle pointed to her chest. "In my heart, I know they are with us."

Charlie wanted so badly to believe that. She'd been fifteen when she lost her parents, and it had torn her apart. What followed had scraped her wounds raw, caused newer, deeper ones. She pushed away the thoughts of their wagon and the agony it brought.

"You think she's here now?" Charlie glanced around as though Maman would pop out from behind the bed with her arms open.

"Of course. They are always with us." Isabelle cupped Charlie's damp cheek. "Draw strength from their love. They surround you with it."

Tears stung Charlie's eyes. "I'm so confused, Iz. I don't know what to do."

Isabelle picked up the comb Charlie had made. The youngest of the boys, Samuel, had inherited his Aunt Charlie's hair. Using her ingenuity and a bone from an elk, she had fashioned a comb with wide teeth to untangle the thickest, curliest hair.

Isabelle moved behind Charlie and started combing. The moment resonated with memories of Maman and for once, it didn't make Charlie sad. It reinforced Isabelle's assertion their parents were always with them.

"Tell me what happened."

Charlie related the story of finding Eli naked, how she had touched his skin, and how much her body had reacted to his.

"I didn't expect it. He's my best friend, not a man."

Isabelle chuckled. "Elijah is a man, I assure you."

"That's not what I meant. He's not a man to me. He's, he's, just... well, just Eli." Charlie was frustrated by the confusion dancing across her mind and heart. "I never thought of him as being male."

Isabelle raised both brows. "Interesting. He's been male since you met him ten years ago. Seeing him naked opened your eyes, so to speak. The question I have is, why did you touch him?"

Charlie's face heated as the memory of how warm his skin was flashed through her mind. "I don't know. He looked so different without his clothes. I never thought about how he looked under his shirt, or his, um, trousers."

"No trousers either, hm?" Isabelle continued to comb Charlie's hair. "You have had an adventure today."

"This isn't funny, Iz. What do I do now? I won't be able to look at him without remembering all of him."

The thought of his beautiful body sent a shiver down hers.

"That, dear sister, is arousal. Passion. It's the magic ingredient to making love. Do you remember Maman's lectures on copulation?" Isabelle spoke so casually of sex, Charlie was embarrassed for her.

"Yes, but I always thought it was disgusting." Charlie's mother had been a nurse and she made sure all of her daughters knew the mechanics of copulation between men and women. None of them would be surprised in the marriage bed, or the premarital bed. At the time, Charlie couldn't imagine wanting to have a man's penis inside her vagina or that it would feel good.

"And now what do you think?" Isabelle started braiding Charlie's hair.

"Do you enjoy it?" Charlie blurted. "I saw his penis and I, uh, wondered. It was big."

"I enjoy it very much. Mason and I have only gotten more passionate over the last ten years. That's how it is with someone you love." Isabelle tied off Charlie's braid with a strip of rawhide, then hugged her quickly. "Sounds to me as though your feelings for Eli have matured into something besides friendship."

Charlie jumped to her feet. "It can't. I mean, I can't. He's my friend. I'm leaving this fort alone and I can't, I just..." She trailed off. Her thoughts whirled around and she couldn't decide whether to be horrified by her reaction or encouraged that she was indeed a female with needs. She thought perhaps that part of her had died ten years earlier. Now she knew it hadn't.

"What you're feeling is normal, Charlie." Isabelle stood. "I've thought for years you were in love with Eli. I am certain he has loved you from the moment he met you and you cursed at him."

Charlie's mouth dropped open. "Love? I don't love him."

"Oh, *chéri*, I think you do, but you have to be the one to accept it, not me." Isabelle kissed her cheek.

"I came here to ask for help, but now you've only confused me more." Charlie wanted to stomp her feet.

"I'm sorry." Isabelle took her hands and squeezed. "My advice to you is to consider the possibility of Eli being more than your friend. What you saw pushed you out of the cocoon of you've hidden in for years. I've been worried you were going to live in that muffled existence forever. I'm happy to hear you are feeling something."

Charlie stared at her sister's beautiful face and wanted to shout at her. The truth was bitter on her tongue, but Isabelle was right. Charlie had been living in a cocoon and she liked it in there. It was comfortable and safe. Eli's naked form had pulled away every layer of protection she had built up around herself.

What was she going to do about it?

Chapter Three

To Charlie's surprise, Eli met her by the edge of the woods in the morning as he'd done too many times to count. She couldn't meet his gaze as she led the gelding by the reins and they walked into the woods together. The familiar act of hunting did little to calm her nerves, but she did it anyway.

"You saw Big Buck?" His voice held only curiosity, nothing of what had transpired the day before. She didn't know if that bothered her or relieved her anxiety.

Her stomach was twisted in knots and she was uncomfortable in his presence for the first time since she'd met him. "Yesterday, I saw some tracks that were too big for the younger bucks. I followed them to a small tributary east of here, and Big Buck was there. I was at least fifteen feet away when he scented me and disappeared, but I saw him." She clenched her free hand into a fist. "I think the bastard smirked."

Eli chuckled and the sound danced across her ears. "He's been hiding from us for five years. I reckon he has a right to smirk."

"Probably be too tough to eat, but I don't care. I want that rack as a trophy, and that hide. It will make a tidy profit. The meat can be used no matter how it tastes." In the dead of winter, salted meat was a commodity sought by every person who lived at the fort.

Eli didn't reply, and the silence stretched between them until it was more than awkward. Charlie should have told him not to bother to meet her, but she couldn't imagine hunting Big Buck without him. He had become a bond between them.

They found a likely tree and climbed, then sat side by side, not talking, uncomfortable and ridiculous, waiting for game to arrive. To her relief, he apparently didn't feel like talking either. She didn't know what was worse—the silence or stilted conversation.

Sweat dripped down Charlie's forehead into her eyes, stinging and unwelcome. She dared not move to wipe her face or even take a breath. A different buck arrived with three does by his side. The elks sipped from a stream, their majestic heads bowed. She had to go for the male, no matter if the females were easier prey. She'd hoped for the damn monster buck, but this one would be a good kill.

Eli remained silent, but his gaze was locked on the animals too. She stared at the creature, its shaggy dark and light fur stark against the green of the spring leaves on the trees. The buck had obviously seen a hard winter, as they all had, and while not skinny, it was definitely not plump. She could wait for another choice, but she would regret it if she didn't take this one down. One of the reasons she hunted in the morning was because she had to dress the carcass, an arduous and lengthy process for a seven hundred pound animal.

"What are you waiting for?" The harsh whisper came from her right.

She turned to glare. "Shut up, Eli."

His bright blue eyes narrowed. "Are you waiting for it to wave its rack at you?"

She huffed out a breath of annoyance and the elk raised its head, ears twitching. Damn Eli for distracting her. He could cost her the kill and the money she could make. When she hunted the big animals, he always came with her. Being a female was a burden sometimes. She accepted her shortcomings, and that included being unable to strap a big kill to a travois by herself. While she was strong, she wasn't that strong.

The image of Eli naked flashed through her mind, and she smashed it. Now was not the time to be distracted or get lost in the what-if game she'd been playing in her head.

Charlie took aim with her bow, the arrow straight and true, nocked to fly. She could hunt with a rifle, but it scared other game. It had taken years, but now she was a better aim with the bow and arrow than a rifle. She held the arrow for a split second before letting it loose. The elk moved as she expected, the arrow finding its mark. The animal died instantly, falling to the forest floor in an elegant heap.

"I can't believe you got him." Eli shook his head. "I thought he was gone for sure."

She let her anger bubble to the surface. It was better than discomfort. "You need to goddamn well shut up when I'm hunting, Eli. I almost lost my shot." She jumped down to the ground, her knees and legs complaining about sitting on a branch for an hour. Charlie shook off the pins and needles as she walked.

Eli loped along behind her. He was a tall man, but his slender form hid hard strength. Now she knew for certain what lay beneath those clothes. He was solid muscle. Sculpted skin and sinew that formed a nearly perfect body. She wasn't one to appreciate a man's form, but damn. Charlie was entranced by Eli's.

It made every word she spoke awkward. Each time she looked at him, she was immediately brought back to the cabin and the sight of his naked form. She'd told him a half truth about seeing only one naked man—Mason, her brother-in-law when he'd been injured, bleeding and covered in dirt. The other man didn't deserve remembering and she shoved the memory away. Eli was clean and deliciously appealing.

Something she never, ever expected. She'd never felt a spark of anything for a man beyond friendship, respect, annoyance or possibly disgust. Now she faced what she didn't want—attraction and arousal.

Charlie walked toward the downed buck with her thoughts heavy. Eli fell into step beside her. She wanted to turn back the clock to when she could have waited for permission to open Eli's door instead of barging in. A silly wish considering it would never come true. She couldn't unsee what she saw, especially since every time she pictured him, her body reacted physically.

Charlie had little experience with men, and at twenty-five, she fully expected to live a life with only her hand for pleasure. Now there was a possibility there could be more. With Eli.

Her mind could barely grasp that possibility. She had no personal knowledge of how passion worked and only the textbook knowledge to make a decision on what to do. It bothered her to be ignorant. Charlie was smart. Her parents had educated each of their four daughters. Hell, her sister Josephine had been a governess when they lived in New York. That was so long ago, Charlie barely remembered the scent, sights and sounds of a city. Now all she knew was Wyoming Territory and the natural world that surrounded her.

Including, apparently, a naked man she had formerly only thought of as a friend, whom Isabelle thought Charlie loved. She could hardly focus as they dressed the elk and loaded it on the travois. Good thing she'd done it hundreds of times so she didn't need to think.

Eli pulled the travois to the waiting horse and attached it with the contraption he'd invented for her years ago. Charlie watched him, intrigued but confused. How did she tell him what she was thinking about? Their friendship had been altered forever the moment she stepped into that cabin.

Charlie used her canteen to clean her hands and knife, then offered it to Eli. He nodded his thanks and washed his own hands. The morning chill had given way to a warmth that spoke of the heat of summer.

She might have suggested a quick dip in the river to finish washing off the blood, but that made her think of Eli dumping water over his wet, nude body. Shit on a shingle. She had to stop thinking about that.

Charlie jerked the reins as she vaulted into the saddle. Her gelding neighed in protest, turning his head and attempting to snack on her leg. Eli gave her a strange look as he took hold of the saddle horn. To her dismay, she almost asked him to walk the five miles back to the fort. How selfish was she? He didn't deserve to be the recipient of her addled wits.

He mounted the horse behind her as he'd done hundreds of times. Today, however, everything had changed. She knew what he looked like beneath the clothes, the beautiful lines of muscle honed by years of hard work. She also knew what his cock looked like, which at rest was quite large. When it had hardened, her curiosity had become rampant need.

To touch, to explore, to know.

Charlie remembered every inch of it, and now it was pressed against her ass. How was she supposed to ride back as if everything was normal? Nothing was normal. It might not ever be again.

Eli tried his damnedest to sit back on the saddle as far as he could. He tried not to touch her, but it was almost impossible. His body ached to do more than rub up against the roundness of her behind. Their easy camaraderie had vanished to be replaced by strained silences. It was all due to the incident in his cabin, when she saw him naked.

The memory of those few minutes had replayed itself over and over in his mind. She'd acted as though she found him attractive. That thought made his body tighten even further.

As they rode the five miles back to the fort, he was surrounded by her scent. She bathed with a soap that smelled of the woods, perhaps made with some wildflowers or herbs. It was her unique smell, one he knew better than he knew his own.

He breathed in deep, pulling her essence into his lungs. Charlie was the one person who would always ground him. His best friend and the woman he'd loved since the moment he'd met her. She had no idea of his feelings and she never would. He had to let the dream go. She would not be his in any other way except as a friend, no matter how he felt about her.

Eli had already started cataloging the women in the fort who were possible wives for him. One stood out from the rest—Jane. She had arrived at the fort last summer with her aunt and uncle, Prudence and Fergus Flanagan. They set up a bakery and sold goods to everyone, including those who passed through the fort. Even Eli's mother, who ran the dining hall for the soldiers, started buying bread from the Flanagans. Jane worked at the bakery. Her dark black hair and bright blue eyes made her the exact opposite of the fiery Charlie.

Jane was sweet, demure and soft-spoken. She had a shy smile and, although pretty, she hadn't allowed any of the single men to do so much as hold her hand. Eli had struck up a conversation with her one day not long after she arrived. Since his heart belonged to Charlie, he offered Jane friendship and to his surprise, she'd reciprocated.

He didn't love her, but he liked her, and that was enough to start a marriage. It was more than his parents had had thirty years ago when they married. Courting Jane was a perfect plan.

Too bad he was still in love with Charlie.

He groaned aloud at his predicament. Charlie turned around, a question in her gaze. Her mouth was inches from him. So very close. Her lips were plump and wet as though she'd just run her tongue along them.

Eli told himself not to touch her. She was his friend, not his lover.

No matter that she'd seen him naked or that he loved her like a crazy man. She was not his to take.

But damn how he wanted to.

He leaned forward that short distance and kissed her. And kissed her. And kissed her. His mouth fused to hers, hot, wet heat that shot a bolt of lightning through his body. He cupped her cheek and ran his tongue along the seam of her lips until she opened her mouth. He dove into heaven, his body disconnected from reason and any thought to consequences. She was softer than he could have ever imagined.

She tasted of peppermint and coffee, as though she'd sucked on a candy after drinking her normal morning beverage. His tongue twined with hers.

Then pain exploded on the side of his head and he was flying through the air. He landed with a bone-jarring thump on the leaf-covered ground. He shook his head to clear the pain and ringing in his ears.

Charlie sat on the saddle, her chin stuck out in a mulish angle he knew well. "Don't ever take from me without asking, Elijah Sylvester."

With that she rode away, regal as a queen, leaving him on the ground. His body ached to kiss her again while his jaw ached with the force of her punch.

Charlie was not meant to be his. If he didn't know it before, he knew it now. So did she. The sooner he courted Jane and got himself a wife, the better things would be.

Chapter Four

Eli wiped his clammy palms on his trousers. Damned if a trickle of sweat wasn't meandering down his spine. It was five thirty in the morning, barely sixty degrees, but he was perspiring like it was a hundred. This morning he was going to start his courtship of Jane.

She didn't know it yet, of course.

His mind was made up, especially after the disastrous kiss with Charlie. His pride—and his ass—still smarted. She'd avoided him for a solid three days. That was hard to do in a place the size of Fort Laramie. She was either hiding in her cabin working or out hunting from sunup to sundown.

No matter what she was doing or where she was, Charlie made it clear she wanted nothing to do with him, both with her reaction to the kiss and with her avoidance. He told himself it was for the best. Ten years of unrequited affection was ridiculous, and he had no one to blame but himself. He was twenty-eight years old, for God's sake. He should have been married with children years ago. Instead he pined after a woman who didn't and wouldn't ever return his love.

He felt stupid and ridiculous. Something he wanted to stop as soon as possible. Thus he woke that morning determined to start wooing Jane. She had already shown an interest in him. He hoped all he would have to do was reciprocate that interest. He had no experience with courtship and he was awkward enough to ruin his chances.

Determined but intimidated, Eli strode toward the bakery. A few soldiers were up patrolling, along with Charlie's sister Isabelle, her shoulders drooping, a medical bag in her hand. She waved at him and he groaned, but he walked over to her.

"Good morning, Eli. You're up early."

"Howdy, Isabelle. I, uh, have a lot to do today. Getting an early start." He toed the dirt, not wanting to meet her gaze.

"Charlie told me what happened." Her tone was full of sympathy and he didn't want it.

Embarrassment heated his cheeks. "She ought not have told personal business to you."

"I'm her sister and she was confused, Eli. There was no other motive. She had a rough time of it ten years ago and it changed her." Isabelle smiled sadly. "She used to skip, sing and dance all the time. I'll bet you didn't know that."

No, he hadn't. The idea of Charlie skipping, dancing and singing was almost ludicrous.

"I'm asking you to be patient with her. She hasn't had a beau and doesn't know what to do around one." Isabelle stifled a yawn behind her hand. "My pardon. I was up all night with a sick patient. I'm for home and some sleep. Fortunately Mason can take care of the boys so I can catch a few hours' rest." She patted his arm. "Good day to you, Eli."

With that Isabelle walked away, leaving him in a more agitated state than he'd been in five minutes earlier. Why did she have to stop and talk to him? He didn't want to know what Charlie had been like. He only knew her now, and the now Charlie wanted nothing to do with him. Eli *had* been patient—hell, he'd wanted to snort at that particular request. Ten years of waiting for Charlie to notice him as a man. Could he have pursued her? Yes, but he didn't want to risk her friendship. Why would he assume she would fall in love with him? He should have said something, but he didn't. Now it was far too late to correct that mistake.

Nope, he was done with Charlie Chastain. He would move on to someone who might actually marry him. Possibly even love him. Whether or not he could love another woman was one more question he didn't know the answer to.

He strode with more speed toward the bakery, which was tucked beside the dining hall. The Flanagans had built quite a business for themselves. With many single men at the fort, the bakery never lacked for business. There were four blue-clad soldiers standing outside chewing on slabs of steaming bread. Eli nodded as he stepped inside, ignoring the whispers of "Fixit".

The smell of the bakery washed over him and he breathed in the deliciousness. The yeasty scent of fresh bread mixed with the sweetness of something else. The warmth of the building felt good after the cool morning air.

Fergus Flanagan was a short, dark-haired man with a friendly disposition. Jane resembled her uncle in some ways, although she probably had her mother's heart-shaped face and blue eyes. Mrs. Flanagan was the toughest of the family, suspicious and curt with most folks.

Fergus was behind the counter, serving the few folks who were inside the bakery. He nodded at Eli and continued with his business until there were no more customers at the counter. He held out a piece of his famous bread slathered with butter. Eli's stomach rumbled and he accepted the offering.

"You know how to draw me in." He smiled and bit into the heavenly concoction. "And you're a wizard at baking. My ma couldn't make bread this good if you paid her a thousand dollars."

Eli's mother, Harriet, was the cook at the dining hall. There wasn't much she couldn't cook well, but she wasn't a good baker. Not even close to what the Flanagans could do.

"What brings you out so early today, Elijah?" Fergus had a thick Irish brogue and a ready smile.

Eli didn't think his tongue would function at all. In fact, he stuttered and then grunted a few times before he crammed another bite of bread in his mouth and smiled crookedly at the man. How was he supposed to tell him he wanted to court Jane? He could hardly accept it himself. It was like putting a raw egg on a plate and trying to keep it steady. Impossible.

"I, ah, have work to do and, uh, I was hungry."

Stupid, stupid, stupid.

"Hey Fixit, whatcha you doing here?" Volner appeared in the doorway, his eyes bloodshot, looking as though he'd spent the night in the pigpen. To Eli's grim satisfaction, Volner still limped a little.

Eli's jaw clenched. He didn't know how to stop the foolish nickname except by ignoring it. Easier to tell himself to do that than to actually do it. What he wanted to do was tell Volner to go to hell.

"Well, ain't you got nothing to say? You ain't no kind of man without your hammer, are ya?" Volner stepped closer, his chest puffed out like a bantam rooster. Eli's hands fisted. "You plan on finishing what you started, Fixit?"

"Stop it, right now, sergeant." Jane stepped between them, her petite form barely topping his shoulder. She put her hands on her hips. "In this bakery, everybody is welcome."

"I ain't meant nothing by it. I was just funning with Fixit." Volner's gaze promised Eli the opposite.

"His name is Elijah. I'm sure my uncle can serve you what you'd like to eat this morning." Jane smiled at the burly sergeant until he moved away, scowling. "Good morning, Eli."

His nervousness faded under her bright personality. She took his arm in her delicate hand. "Uncle Fergus gave you some bread already. Would you like coffee to go with it?" Her voice was sweet and light with a hint of brogue. She likely never had a curse word pass her pink lips. Who wouldn't want to marry this lovely lady and see her face every morning and night?

"Coffee sounds perfect." Eli smiled back at her, sure his idea to court this young lady was the right one.

He ignored the little voice deep inside that told him he was wrong. So very wrong.

Charlie sat in the corner of the dining hall alone. After avoiding Eli for three days, she was lonely and crankier than she had been. She began to think of her life as before-Eli-naked and before-Eli-kiss. Each event had sent her spinning in circles that she hadn't yet recovered from.

Not that she knew how to recover.

Isabelle had tried her best to offer advice, but Charlie still felt as though she were afloat in a turbulent sea alone. There were days when she forgot what it was like to have a mother. Then there were days she missed Maman so much she nearly puked.

Ten years later and Charlie was a fifteen-year-old orphan in the body of a twenty-five-year-old woman. Caught in the transition from child to adult without someone to guide her, Charlie struggled to make choices that most people took for granted. She knew it, but she had no idea how to solve it. The only avenue seemed to be "the plan". Leaving the fort would grant her anonymity and freedom living amongst people would never provide.

Her whirling thoughts left her miserable, eating her supper without tasting a bite of it.

"Good evening, Miss Chastain."

Charlie looked up from cutting her ham to find Captain Hamilton towering over her. He held his flat-brimmed hat in his hand, and to her surprise, he was crushing it. Like he was nervous. Because of her? Impossible.

"Captain."

He gestured to the table at which she sat. "Do you mind if I join you for the evening meal?"

Her impulse was to tell him no. She didn't want company. She didn't deserve it. However, when she opened her mouth, she said, "I suppose that's all right."

He smiled and her stomach did a flip. She blinked at both the handsome visage of the man and her reaction. What had Eli done to her? She never looked at a man as a *man* until she'd seen what was beneath Eli's clothes. He'd then had the balls to kiss her. She did him a favor by not shooting him, although she really, really wanted to.

Now she was turning into a…a female.

The captain returned with a plate of food and sat down. He shook out a napkin with a snap and placed it on his lap. She watched him, frozen in place by the revelation that she found him attractive. Her. Charlotte Chastain, the toughest woman in the territory. What the fucking hell was going on?

He set his hat down on the bench beside him and then looked up at her. The captain had nice blue eyes and russet-colored hair, with a matching mustache. He was not much older than her, if not younger. His skin was still pale from wherever he'd come from. Being out in the territory gave everyone enough time in the sun and wind to cause coarse skin. This soldier was too pretty to be a captain of the rough soldiers at the fort.

"Thank you for letting me join you." He waited until he chewed and swallowed before he spoke. Definitely a gentleman.

She shrugged. "The dining hall is open to everyone. It's not my table."

"Still, since you're alone, I didn't want to make you uncomfortable."

She snorted. "Not likely, captain."

"Kenneth. My name is Kenneth." There was that smile again.

"Well, Kenneth, I should probably tell you about me since you seem to think I'm a lady or at least a decent female." She watched his reaction, which was only a tiny widening of his eyes.

"Go on."

"I wear britches every day. Haven't worn a dress in at least seven years and don't plan on it, no matter what my sister thinks. I cuss. A goddamn lot. I make my living by hunting for others, then I sell the skin, sinew, bones, hooves and any other part of the animal I can make useful. I'm in blood up to my elbows half the time." She took a bite of her ham and deliberately spoke as she chewed. Let him see the full effect of all that was Charlie Chastain.

Kenneth wiped his mouth with the napkin. "I know all this about you."

Charlie scowled and swallowed the bite in her mouth. "How?" Her gut clenched. Had he been spying on her?

He shrugged. "I asked people and I spoke to your sister. I also met you already, if you remember."

She waved her hand in dismissal. "Fine. Why did you follow me and ask questions about me? I'm not pretty. I'm cranky and as unfemale as you can be and still have tits. So tell me why."

At this, his gaze dropped to his plate. She had the sinking feeling he'd made a bet and she was the prize. Or he was going to ask her to butcher a cow for him. Or something equally as awful.

"I grew up in Philadelphia, the son of a wealthy banker. I had all the privileges and advantages I could ever want." His mouth twisted. "I hated it."

She rolled her eyes at that piece of foolishness. "Of course you did. 'Cause living out here in the west is much better than a fancy mansion with servants."

This time he frowned. "It's better for me. There's freedom so wide and deep I can taste it." His expression grew animated and to her surprise, more handsome. Appealing.

"That still doesn't explain why you asked about me or why the hell you're sitting here with me." Charlie wasn't angry at him, but she was damn well frustrated.

"I like you."

She narrowed her gaze. "Again, why?"

He cocked his head, his blue eyes thoughtful. "You don't think very much of yourself."

That particular barb hit too close. She pointed at his food. "Eat your food and shut up or get the hell out of here."

He should be insulted. He should get up and walk away, then stay away. Instead, he went back to eating. Charlie stared open-mouthed. What was wrong with this man? Was he stupid or a glutton for punishment?

"You have lovely eyes." He scooped a forkful of beans into his mouth. "Although your face is the most striking feature you have."

Charlie's stomach bounced up to her throat and then down to her feet, landing with a splat. No one had ever called her lovely or striking. Kenneth must be blind, stupid and foolish.

"You can't possibly mean that."

He frowned. "I don't lie. I joined the military because of my belief in justice and truth. There are too many people who spend their time lying to themselves and everyone else. I might be a fool for telling you what I think, and I might do something stupid like try to kiss you, but I do not lie."

Charlie couldn't speak. Her voice had flitted away at his words. Kiss her? How had the world spun sideways in a week where not one but two men wanted to kiss her? She believed Kenneth. There were few people in the world she trusted or believed. Somehow she believed the captain told her the truth. She still didn't know why.

Before she could rethink her action, she picked up the knife beside her plate and speared his sleeve to the table. To his credit, he only blinked and met her gaze.

"I hope you can mend that hole." He frowned.

"Why are you here and why have you gathered information about me? No more shit, Kenneth." She spoke through her teeth, emotion making her voice thick. She didn't want this man to cause a reaction inside her. Keeping herself safe from everyone was too important. He had broken through her defenses without a fight.

"You intrigue me. You're not like the rest of the women here. You're tough, no-nonsense, and you know one end of a gun from the other." He met her gaze. "The perfect soldier's wife."

Holy shit.

Chapter Five

Eli buttoned up his best shirt and tucked it into his trousers. He ran his hands down the fabric and wished he had a mirror to see how he looked. All his life, he'd avoided his reflection—until he decided to marry Jane. Now he wanted to be sure he looked his best.

It shouldn't matter how he was dressed, but it did. Eli had scratched out his living since he was a child. He cleaned, carried and delivered whatever he could manage to heft into his arms. When his father died almost fifteen years ago, Eli had to become a man even if he barely had a whisker on his chin. His mother had no one except Eli and he had no other option but to work. His education had been minimal, but he could read, write and cipher.

His father had died on their way to Oregon, and like Charlie and her sister, Eli and his mother had to choose to settle in the Wyoming Territory or buck the odds to try to make it the rest of the way alone. His mother was tiny in stature but tough as hell. She got a job working in the kitchen of the eating establishment at what was then Fort John. Now she ran the dining hall, planned the meals and managed the other two kitchen workers.

Eli started by cleaning the slop bucket, sweeping floors, digging outhouses and shoveling horse shit. It wasn't until he fixed the well head pump that he caught the eye of Mr. Johnson, who had run many of the areas of the fort until the army took over. It was Mr. Johnson who first called Eli "Fixit", and the moniker stuck.

He knew he was quiet and a bit of a loner. Except for Charlie, he'd never truly had a friend before. He was also tall and slender. No matter how strong he was, he appeared as though he ate nothing, which was far from the truth. He ate a lot. All the time. Yet he remained thin. He'd been compared to a hammer or a nail, as well as a sapling.

None of it flattering and all of it annoying and, if he were honest with himself, it chipped away at his confidence. As he grew older, he tried to shake the damn nickname, but it hung around his neck like an albatross.

Now he was a grown man, almost thirty years old. He was happy with his job, enjoyed fixing things. When something broke or needed to be built, he would "see" what needed to be done and then follow the plan he created in his head. No one understood it, but that didn't matter. He did and he was damn good at something he liked to do.

It wasn't all good days, though. Sometimes he still had to clean horse shit or shovel snow. And sometimes bastards like Volner and Oxley needled him until he couldn't see straight. His temper had always bubbled beneath the surface, but now he let it fly. There was immense satisfaction when he defended himself.

He wasn't the best catch as far as husbands went, but he was better than many. He could support a family and he was frugal with his money. If he wasn't handsome or big as an ox, well, that was the way things went. He would treat a wife well and he would do his level best to be sure she never wanted for anything.

Eli stepped out into the evening air and took a deep breath then let it out slowly through his mouth. He was escorting Jane to supper for the first time. He strode toward the dining hall, determined to enjoy his meal and the lovely company.

Jane insisted on meeting him there and Eli wondered if it had anything to do with her aunt. Mrs. Flanagan hated everyone, but she seemed to truly dislike Eli. Winning the older woman over would be the biggest hurdle to marrying her niece.

He saw Jane waiting by the door. The petite brunette was surrounded by three soldiers. Eli hurried, sure he was late when he intended to be early. Next time he'd insist on meeting her at the bakery.

"Evening, gentlemen." Eli strode through them, his height an advantage he was grateful for. The soldiers glanced up at him, their expressions wary. "Miss Flanagan, I'm sorry I'm late." He held out his arm. Her hand was cold and shaky as she tucked it into the crook of his elbow.

Damn. He wanted to kick himself.

"Mr. Sylvester." She nodded regally at the soldiers and walked into the dining hall with her head high and shoulders straight.

"I'm sorry I was late." He spoke softly.

"You weren't. I was early." Twin spots of color ran high on her cheeks. "I was a bit anxious, I expect."

"Why would you be anxious?" Eli blurted before his brain could stop his runaway mouth.

She glanced down and smiled. "I've been waiting near on a year for you to notice me, Elijah. You spend all your time working or with that hunter lady."

At this he felt his own cheeks heat. "Charlie is my best friend." Damn but he needed to practice speaking like a regular person and not a fool.

"I'm glad you have a best friend. I'm more glad you're having supper with me instead of her." Jane gestured to her right. "Seems that she's also spending time with other folks too."

Eli stumbled when he spotted Charlie across the table from Captain Hamilton. The officer had made it clear he was interested in marrying her. He had been serious about his pursuit of Charlie. It shouldn't bother Eli at all. He'd decided his infatuation with her was behind him. His heart and his head didn't necessarily follow the same path, however.

His gut clenched hard enough he tasted bile in the back of his throat. Charlie appeared as though she was enjoying her meal and the company.

She was not for him. She was not his. She never would be.

Eli dug deep for a smile. "Are you hungry? Let's sit over here." He led Jane to the opposite side of the dining hall and sat with his back to Charlie. He couldn't look at her and still be able to swallow.

He was a complete fool.

Charlie was more than surprised to find herself relaxing in Kenneth's company. He was smart, and had a dry sense of humor. His looks were classically handsome and he had the whitest teeth she'd ever seen on another human being. Kenneth had returned her knife handle first. He'd surprised her again.

And apparently he wanted to court her. To marry her.

She was still reeling from the knowledge. She should get up and leave—after all, marrying someone wasn't part of "the plan". Yet she sat there and ate her supper.

The week had started with seeing Eli naked, then he kissed her, and now Kenneth. What had set the world on a sideways spin?

As she sipped at her coffee, she glanced across the dining hall and spotted the very man who had kicked her life into that spin. He was sitting down to a table with a little girl. Charlie tried to see who the girl was, but Eli blocked her view. It wasn't her business if he had a meal. A man had to eat, and he did eat as if he had a hollow leg.

"Something wrong?" Kenneth eyed her with far too much insight.

"None of your business." She spoke without rancor. Her temper had cooled during her time with the captain. He had a calming effect on her. Unexplainable.

He looked behind him and eyed the dining room occupants, then turned back. "Mr. Sylvester."

Far too perceptive. She shrugged.

"I've heard he's called Fixit."

Charlie scowled. "That's not his name and using it is an insult."

Kenneth held up his hands. "I haven't used that name. I was merely making an observation."

"Stick your observation up your ass." She waited for him to huff and puff, then walk away.

He didn't. "You care for him, then. Is he my rival for your affections?"

What did she tell him since she wasn't sure how she felt? Eli was just about the most important person in her life. She hadn't spoken to him in three days. That was why things were sideways. She missed him.

"Eli is my best friend." She didn't offer any other explanation. It wasn't his business, but she understood why he asked. If Kenneth truly wanted to marry her, something she still had trouble believing, then he would have to accept Eli was part of her life. Not that she was staying at the fort or marrying anyone.

"Unusual." He gestured behind him. "Is he courting Miss Flanagan?"

Charlie stared at him, her heart thumping. "What did you say?"

"Miss Flanagan. She's having supper with Mr. Sylvester. I considered courting her, but she appears too meek for the wife of a soldier." Kenneth chewed as she tried to absorb his words.

Charlie was on her feet and walked toward Eli before she knew what she was doing. Her heart hadn't stopped whomping on her ribs since Kenneth had said the woman's name. Charlie knew who she was. The tiny little woman whose family owned the bakery. She'd kept her distance from Charlie, her large eyes fearful whenever they saw each other. Charlie had shrugged off the woman's reaction since many new females to the fort treated her the same way.

Now the pretty little thing was having a meal with Eli. Charlie wasn't jealous—she was confused. And hurt. She marched up to the table, ignoring Miss Flanagan's wide-eyed expression. Eli's back was to Charlie, but he stiffened.

Miss Flanagan swallowed hard. "M-miss Chastain, will you join us?"

Eli spoke. "She has a supper companion, Jane. I'm sure she's too busy."

Charlie counted to ten until she trusted herself to speak. She had been lucky enough to have parents and sisters who loved her unconditionally. She had also started her life with happiness and safety. However, the journey west had shown her true evil and the darkest of dark souls. She'd been hurt physically, emotionally and mentally, enough that the scars had never truly healed.

Since that time she'd let very few people into her life and even few into her heart. Eli had been allowed access to both. He had now betrayed that trust and caused new slashes in her heart.

She wanted to punch him, make him feel the same pain she did. How dare he treat her as though she didn't matter?

"Elijah." Her voice was as rough as though she'd been gargling rocks.

"Outside. Now."

She wouldn't embarrass any of them by pitching a fit in the dining room. Out of the corner of her eye, she saw his mother, Harriet, watching them with a frown on her face. Harriet had been like a favorite aunt, always kind to Charlie. The dining room was Eli's mother's domain and Charlie couldn't disrespect her by causing a scene.

Eli still hadn't looked at Charlie. "I just sat down to eat. I'm sure Jane wants to eat her food warm."

Charlie leaned down and whispered in his ear. "If you don't get your fucking ass up, I will do more than make your goddamn food cold."

He huffed out a breath but stood. "I'll be right back, Jane."

Jane managed a shaky smile, but her eyes were wide as saucers. No doubt life in a bakery wasn't exciting or dangerous, unlike Charlie's, which was full of both. Yet she never quenched her thirst for more. Perhaps nothing ever would.

She marched out the door, not bothering to see if he followed. He wouldn't dare not to. The cool night air felt good on her overheated skin. Her fists clenched and she told herself not to punch him. It would only serve to make the situation worse and convince him she was as crazy as everyone said she was.

"What do you want, Charlie?" His voice was not as unaffected as he pretended to be.

She tried to push aside the hurt, but it proved too difficult. A ball of pain lodged in her chest and she pushed against it, trying to force it away. "You kissed me three days ago. Tonight I see you in the dining hall with that woman."

"Sounds about right." His tone was flat.

"How dare you?" She poked a finger in his chest. "You kissed me like a man does a woman, turn my world upside down and then you throw me away as though I'm easily replaced." The ache sounded through her words.

"You didn't seem to like the kisses, Charlie. I seem to remember you punching me and throwing me to the ground." He finally sounded upset. Good.

"You didn't ask my permission." She wanted to punch him again. "I've had people take what they want from me without asking. As I told them no and fought. I will never let someone take from me again."

Dark memories surged up her throat, choking her. Flashes of Camille and Karl and then pain. Bile coated the back of her throat.

Before she realized it, Charlie was on her knees retching into the dirt. Shame took over the anger she'd been struggling with. Eli handed her a handkerchief and rubbed her back. Thankfully he didn't say anything, but he did block everyone's view of her pitiful display of weakness.

She was finally able to sit back on her haunches and take a breath. Eli crouched beside her, silent. She wiped her eyes on her sleeve.

"I'm sorry." His soft apology was heartfelt.

"I would have said yes." She struggled to her feet. "I would have said yes if you had asked. Now you've tossed that away."

Charlie's heart broke into a thousand pieces as she walked away from him. She felt his gaze on her back. Why did it feel as though part of her life had ended? He was the most important person in her life and now everything had changed.

Chapter Six

Several weeks passed in a blur of work and courting. Eli spent two suppers, one picnic by the river and five afternoon walks with Jane. It was typical courtship, and Jane appeared happy as any girl with a beau. She smiled prettily and laughed at all of Eli's jokes.

He should be as happy as Jane. Thrilled to have a woman think him worthy of her affection and eventually, her love.

Instead all he could think of was Charlie's face when she accused him of taking from her without permission, of her obvious pain as she crouched on the ground and vomited. It broke his heart to see her in agony. He'd wanted to hold her until she expunged the pain that had taken over her.

Eli had to cease pining for Charlie. She made it very clear he had broken trust with her and there would be no forgiveness. He'd made a terrible mistake and he wanted to turn back the clock and undo it, unkiss her, unbreak the moment he'd lost her.

Foolish to yearn for a woman who had only considered him a friend, the assistant who helped her cart around her kills. He knew she had made him a part of her life, but nothing more. No matter how much he had regrets about what he'd done or hadn't done, he had to put Charlie and any future with her behind him.

He had a beautiful girl on his arm. One who made him feel ten feet tall with her petite form. Jane barely came to his shoulder and was delicate enough he thought he might break her if he grew too amorous. He would have to bend at the waist just to kiss her.

She was sweet and funny and a lovely person. Eli looked down at her tiny hand on his long arm and wondered what she saw in him. He'd been compared to a scarecrow, tall, thin and gangly. His face wasn't handsome either. The first time any woman had seemed to consider him attractive had been when Charlie saw him naked. He had to push aside that memory or it would spoil his time with Jane.

"Summer is definitely arriving." Jane shaded her eyes and looked up at the clear blue sky. "We'll have to take our walks in early morning or evening soon." This was said with a shy smile.

"That sounds nice." His words were wooden even to his own ears.

Jane, as expected, was no fool. She stopped and frowned up at him, her eyes clouded with confusion. "You know, when I first noticed you I wondered if you were married to Miss Chastain. You spent so much time together, it was a natural assumption. Then when I found out the truth, I thought perhaps you were courting her, but that didn't seem to be the case either. I am genuinely fond of you, Elijah. I hope there is something there between us, and maybe one day you can be fond of me too."

With that, Jane left him standing on his own. To her credit, she kept her head high and walked at a steady pace back to the bakery. He deserved it and more.

The big man, Gunther, who had worked at the fort on and off the last ten years, watched him from the shadows behind the bakery. There was history there between him and the Chastain sisters, but Eli had not had more than the most cursory conversations with him. The man was the size of an ox and he could, quite literally, break Eli in half.

As frightening as his countenance was, Gunther had never threatened anyone or anything. He simply worked like ten men and spent the rest of his time somewhere alone.

Eli wanted to run to the big man and force him to reveal what he knew of Charlie. How he would accomplish that was a mystery. Before he could do anything, Gunther disappeared behind one of the buildings. Damn.

Eli was torn by what his heart and his head told him. He'd never been in such a strange situation before and he wanted to find someone to talk to about it. Not Charlie or her sister Isabelle, and for certain not his mother. That left him with only one choice.

Charlie didn't know what she was thinking when she accepted Kenneth's invitation to go walking that evening. She'd never stepped out with a man in her life, much less doing something as highfalutin as to "go walking".

After they'd eaten supper together again, he held out his arm like a real gentleman and to her surprise, she put her hand through the crook of his elbow like a real lady. It was all falsehood on her part. Charlie was in no way a lady in form, word or deed. Yet Kenneth seemed to ignore all of that.

It puzzled her and confused her, which in turn intrigued her. She wasn't accustomed to finding anything interesting, let alone a man. He was smart and polite with hints of a sense of humor. Most of all he was a soldier, very disciplined and in control at all times. She'd never known anyone like him.

His wool coat was stiff beneath her hand, but solid and warm. She didn't get a crick in her neck looking at him like she did Eli. Kenneth was only four or five inches taller than her. He always smelled good, like soap and something she suspected was hair pomade. Being someone with hair that tended to frizz and turn into a cloud of knots, she understood the draw of using something to tame it. Kenneth had red hair, which was more of a carrot color than hers. It was always perfectly coifed, which said something about his ironclad control.

Charlie was free as the wind, never conforming or keeping anything within limits. That would stifle her. "How do you not go crazy?"

His eyebrows drew together. "Pardon me?"

She gestured to his uniform. "All of this. How do you not go crazy? Too many rules, people telling you what to do, where to go, how to dress." She made a face. "I couldn't do it."

Kenneth smiled, reminding her how handsome he was. His mustache curled up at the corners. "I prefer to have that control. It helps me focus."

"I don't understand that. I would spend so much time trying to conform, I'd lose all pleasure from doing what I do."

He patted her hand. "My career is not for pleasure. I thrive in an orderly environment. Without the Army, I wouldn't be the man I am."

"I suppose I wouldn't be who I am without my hunting either." She mused about what she would be doing if she weren't at the fort. Her mind drew a blank.

"I've heard you have the skills of a native hunter, ah, and deliver as promised." He was funny when he tried to speak of her violent profession as respectable. It was charming.

"I enjoy what I do. I couldn't be all stiff and disciplined." She watched a few soldiers running drills in the corner of the fort.

He chuckled. "You are more disciplined than I am."

Charlie stopped dead in her tracks. "What in the blue hell are you talking about?"

"With your hunting, you are exceptionally disciplined. You track, stalk and sit for quite some time waiting for game, don't you? Dressing a kill, tanning a hide, butchering the meat. It's all very disciplined." He spoke calmly as though he wasn't tearing her world apart.

The very idea what she did was disciplined, that she was controlled, shocked her to her very core. "I never thought of it that way."

"It's one of the reasons I was drawn to you." Kenneth continued to speak with such frankness.

"You like me because I sit in a tree for two hours without having to piss?"

A laugh burst from his throat. "You never cease to surprise me."

"Good. I sure as hell don't want to be boring." Charlie found her own mouth turning up in a grin. What was it about this stiff Army captain that appealed to her? He was very different from Eli, couldn't be more different. She missed her best friend, but Kenneth did bring an element of new into her life.

"*You* are anything but boring." Kenneth looked up into the darkening sky. "One of these days I would truly like to kiss you."

Oh hell.

"If you try it without my say-so, you'll get yourself a black eye for the effort." She wasn't allowing Kenneth to take without her permission either. Damn men thought they could do whatever they want.

"I would never." Kenneth scowled, looking affronted she would even suggest such a thing.

"Glad we're in agreement on that."

"I'm a soldier and a gentleman." He straightened his shoulders, a seemingly impossible task since they were as straight as a razor already.

"That doesn't make a damn bit of difference. I've seen self-proclaimed gentlemen act like rutting stags after a female in heat." Charlie didn't know why she was being so fractious. Kenneth had been well behaved, but that didn't meant she wouldn't be on her guard.

"You do have a unique way of expressing yourself."

She shrugged. "I'm not gonna apologize for being me."

At this he smiled. "One of the reasons you intrigued me is your abundance of self-confidence."

Charlie turned away so he wouldn't see the color in her cheeks. Self-confidence? She had so little of it, she was surprised he would assume she had any. Instead he thought she had a lot. An "abundance". A ridiculous bubble of laughter threatened to erupt from her throat. She was only brave when her loved ones were in danger. Otherwise she hid from the world.

Kenneth didn't know who she was. Not really. He saw what she showed the world. That was no fault of his own. She didn't let anyone see the true Charlie. If he wanted to court her, he should recognize she wasn't who he saw on the outside.

Disappointment speared her heart. Perhaps he would never see beyond the shell that protected her.

Charlie had never been so lonely in her life. She had Isabelle to talk to, but between raising three boys, teaching music to a few children, and her patients, Iz had little time to listen to her sister's troubles. There was no one else close by. Her other sisters, Josephine and Francesca, lived three days' ride southwest. Charlie could write to them, but they would know something was wrong, then leave their children to race to the fort.

The last thing Charlie wanted was more fuss made about her. She had successfully avoided Eli and Jane for two weeks. Kenneth had come to see her on numerous occasions, escorting her to supper several times. He'd even brought her a bouquet of wildflowers. The captain was doing everything right and people at the fort noticed his attention. Too bad she saw nothing beyond a nice man who didn't know her at all.

Some of the ladies who had previously stuck their noses in the air when Charlie walked past had started to greet her or nod in passing. It was strange to be accepted after ten years of being ignored—or worse, treated with disdain. Now because she had become of interest to the man who ran the fort, she was socially different. That left a bad taste in her mouth.

It was a beautiful late spring morning and the sun had just started to pain the sky in hues of pink and orange. She rode her gelding into the woods beyond the fort alone. Eli hadn't accompanied her on every hunting trip she'd taken, but she still felt his absence.

She missed him.

Eli had been a part of her life for ten years. Leaving him behind for good made her heart ache. Their last encounter had yanked dark moments from behind the closed door of her memories. She'd hardly slept in the two weeks since and when she did, nightmares clawed at her.

Kenneth had already remarked on her appearance, the bags beneath her eyes and her haggard face. Charlie wasn't pretty to start with and right about then, she was downright scary-looking.

The birds sang into the clear morning air, squirrels chattered and nearby a dog barked. It was idyllic and perfect. If only it was as calm inside her soul.

Her bow sat on her back, comfortable and familiar. The horse beneath her was also comforting. Yet the space behind her reminded her that her life had changed yet again.

"You need help?" The male voice startled her and she reached for the pistol on her hip.

Gunther stood near a tree, his expression guarded. He'd never spoken to her in the ten years since she'd been held captive by his mother and brother. True to his word, he'd left her and Isabelle alone. His face was as ugly as it had been years ago, during the harsh winter that almost broke her. He was the one person at the fort who was more alone than she was.

"What do you want?" Her voice was as sharp as the knife in her boot.

He shrugged. "You're hunting without the tall man."

"That's none of your business." She was dismayed to realize everyone knew she and Eli had had a falling out.

"I thought you might need help." He gestured to the woods. "The tall man usually helps you."

"You've been watching me?" She cocked the gun, her hand shaking with the rage she'd bottled up inside for so long. "You have a death wish?"

"No, I promised your sister I would watch over you."

This was news to her. Isabelle trusted him to watch over Charlie? That was startling.

"I don't believe you."

His massive shoulders moved again. She lowered the pistol. Even now his posture was defeated. There had never been anything aggressive in his behavior toward her when she'd been captive. He hadn't hurt her and he'd done what he could to protect Isabelle. He was physically powerful, but it seemed his mother had drained him of any aggression.

Or perhaps it was all a ruse. The Beckers were very skilled at deceit.

Charlie shook her head. "Nope, I can't and I won't believe you, Gunther. You'd best be on your way."

He nodded, accepting her decision before he lumbered off into the woods.

It wasn't the companionship she wanted, and she would remain alone. As pitiful as it was, she had considered accepting his offer. The very man who reminded her of the nightmare of her past. Her life had become a sad parody of what it could be and she didn't know how to change it.

She headed out on her own, her thoughts troubled and distracted. More than likely her hunt would yield nothing, but she didn't want to be at the fort today. There were too many reminders of what she wanted to avoid.

When the sound of twigs snapping sounded behind her, she stopped. "I told you no, Gunther. Do I need to spell it for you?" She turned to find two soldiers behind her, smirking. The pistol was in her hand in the blink of an eye. While her heart pounded, Charlie remained outwardly calm. Being a hunter had put her in many dangerous situations and she never lost control. At least not with an animal. These two men fell into that category.

"What do you want?"

"Where's your man?" The tall one—his name was Volner—eyed her with a greasy smile.

"I don't have a man. I take care of myself." She gestured toward where the fort lay. "I'm sure you have some soldiering to do."

"Nope. We're off duty." Volner scratched his balls. She wondered what kind of critters lived in that particular hellhole.

"What do you want?" She slid the knife from the sheath on her back. If they decided to attack, she would have a fighting chance.

"Oxley wants company."

She snorted. "You came to the wrong girl for that. I hear Rosie's got a whorehouse about ten miles east of here."

"He don't want to pay for nothing and I'm here to make sure he don't." Volner stepped closer and her hand tightened on the hilt of the knife.

"Then you got a palm and five fingers." She cocked the pistol. "Get moving."

Volner moved to the right and the fat one to the left. Charlie knew a moment of fear, and she was a helpless child again for that moment. She pushed aside her weakness and hardened herself. Her muscles poised to fight for her life.

"Fixit ain't here to protect you. I hear he's been keeping company with that little bitty thing. She ain't gonna give him the ride you would." Volner nodded at his friend and they flanked her.

Her finger tightened on the trigger and she prepared to kill her first human being.

Chapter Seven

Eli found Mason hunched over his desk in the small school, no doubt in preparation for the day. Charlie's brother-in-law had been a university professor from North Carolina who had chased gold west only to end up near death somewhere on the trail to Oregon. Fortunately for him, the Chastain sisters had found him and nursed him back to health.

He'd married Isabelle and now had three beautiful children as well. Mason had always been kind to Eli but not condescending. Unlike many of the other men in the fort, he treated Eli like an equal, no matter Mason's upper-class background and breeding.

"Good morning." Mason smiled. "It's always a sincere pleasure to see you, Eli. What brings you to my domain?"

Eli looked at Mason's earnest gaze and sat on a bench with a bone-jarring thump. His throat tightened. "I'm in love with Charlie." The words tumbled out without a shred of control.

"This is not news. I believe it's been apparent for many years." Mason looked apologetic. "The only person who didn't appear to acknowledge this was you."

Misery made Eli's shoulders slump. "She doesn't see me."

Mason closed the book in his hand. "Charlotte refuses to see anything beyond her own despair. She endured much on the journey west and she hasn't yet escaped the shadows that hold her captive. Isabelle despairs her sister will ever emerge into the light."

"What happened to her?" Eli couldn't stop himself from asking. "A few weeks ago, she, um, puked over a memory, but she wouldn't tell me what it was. And she hasn't talked to me since."

Mason stared hard at Eli. "Charlotte is a very private person. She does not let many into her world, but she allowed you in. When she is ready, she will tell you what she can. Do not expect her to reveal all."

"I just want her to talk to me again. I miss her." Eli didn't know how to even get close enough to talk to her. "I thought if I married someone else, I could put her out of my heart."

Mason shook his head. "Elijah, you cannot flush love from your heart. Once embedded, it will never let loose, no matter what."

"That's what I was afraid of." Eli put his head in his hands. "I've made a mess of things."

Mason cleared his throat. "I believe that's an understatement."

"What do I do?" Eli heard the desperation in his voice and hated it. It reminded him of Fixit, the gangly fool who could hardly get out of his own way. Eli was a man now, stronger than the boy he'd been so long ago. Just like Charlie was not the girl she was, but that didn't mean she was less. It meant she was more.

"Apologize for being an idiot. Ladies do appreciate a man who can grovel." Mason smiled. "The good news is I believe Charlotte returns the love you have for her. It's going to be a difficult task for her to accept it. Especially if you're courting Jane Flanagan."

Eli's cheeks heated. "Jane would be a good wife."

"I don't disagree, but would she make you a good wife?" Mason narrowed his gaze. "You have to choose your own path, Elijah. It may feel as though you're chewing rocks when you make that choice. However, your heart will know when it's the right one."

Eli scowled. "That's not helpful."

"I can't tell you what your path is. You are the only one who can do that." Mason tented his fingers. "I spent the first part of my life indulging in the vices of the rich, thinking I was above others, drinking and whoring. Then I almost died and was reborn as the man you see before you. Better than I was? Maybe, but decidedly different. My advice is to make a choice you won't regret."

Eli didn't think he would become a whole different person if he married Jane. She was a sweet woman who no man could fault as a mate. But the problem was, she wasn't Charlie. No matter how he tried to convince himself to forget her, his heart always returned to the woman who didn't want him.

"Don't despair, Elijah." Mason leaned forward and patted Eli's shoulder. "You have mettle. Stand strong and have faith in how you feel."

"That's what I've been doing for ten years. Waiting for her to see how I felt." Eli got to his feet, too agitated to sit still. "Then I kissed her—"

"Wait a moment, she let you kiss her?" Mason's brows nearly touched his hairline.

Eli stared out the window on the wall. "Not exactly. I kissed her, but she didn't let me. Ended up on my ass with a sore jaw."

Mason laughed. "That sounds like the little one I know."

"She's not so little. And her fist is as hard as a hammer." Eli clenched his hands. "She made it clear she doesn't want me around. I know I ain't a catch, but I would always take care of her, love her."

Mason stepped up beside him. "Maybe she doesn't need to be taken care of. Perhaps what she wants is someone to respect her many skills and love her for who she is, no matter how different she is."

Eli blinked. "I do respect her and love her. I don't want her to change."

"Have you informed her of these important facts?"

"No. I reckon I should've done that." Eli was smart, but sometimes he was dumb as a bag of rocks. How could Charlie know what he felt if he never told her?

Idiot.

Charlie told her arms to stay straight and true, her weapons firmly pointed at the rat bastards. Her finger itched to tug on the trigger, to end the sons of bitches who thought it a good idea to intimidate her. She had no doubt they meant her harm. What she didn't know was why.

The fat one tripped over anything near his feet. He wouldn't be a problem. The taller man would be the one to watch. He had a deadness in his eyes, one she recognized from another man, Karl Becker, who along with his mother Camille and Gunther stole their wagon and held her family hostage. The evil man and his equally evil mother had done more damage in the short time Isabelle and Charlie had been their captives than any human being should have.

She shook off the memories that crawled up her throat then tightened her grip on the pistol. She had one chance to hit her mark, and if she didn't, there was always the knife. However, she was realistic enough to recognize she didn't have much of a chance to overpower them. She had to outthink them and outsmart them.

"You want a hole in your head?" She stepped backward, keeping her back to the forest. Damn good thing she'd spent years exploring because she knew right where she was. There was a ditch about ten feet behind her and if she were lucky, they would fall into it before realizing it was there.

For the first time in two weeks, she let herself miss Eli. He hunted with her often and if she hadn't been angry at him, he would be there now.

"Nope, I want to have fun." The tall one grinned.

"Why me? I'm no siren made to tempt men." She made it another three feet.

"I don't fucking care what you look like." He flipped his hand in dismissal and she told her gut not to clench. It didn't listen. "I want you because of what you mean to him."

She didn't need to ask who "him" was. "Why do you care what Eli feels?"

"Fixit is a little shit. He thinks he can do whatever the hell he wants, but he can't. I am going to make him regret going up against me." The man grinned, revealing yellowed teeth that resembled a wolf's fangs more than a human mouth. "After I'm done with you, you won't forget me."

"Yes I will, you fucking idiot." She sneered at him. "Because I don't give a shit who you are. I'm also going to kill you."

The man blinked before he appeared to shake off her threat. "Feel free to call out my name when I fuck you."

He moved closer, but his gaze flickered to her left. Too late: she had forgotten about the shorter man, and his fist crashed into the side of her face. Stars danced across her vision as the coppery taste of blood coated her mouth.

She squeezed the trigger as she fell. Cursing exploded heavenward as the smell of gunpowder lit the air. She barely felt the ground as she slammed against it. She tried not to lose consciousness, but blackness roared through her. She thought she heard fists crunching against flesh, and then she knew no more.

Chapter Eight

Eli carried a few boards toward the fence around the guardhouse at the gate to the fort. Some drunk fool had a fight with another drunk fool and they had both landed at the fence, splintering a few boards. It wasn't the first time, it wouldn't be the last.

The morning air was heavy with the scent of summer flowers the officers' wives planted. The sounds of a normal day echoed around him, including soldiers running drills, dogs barking, a few women chatting as they hung laundry. All of it familiar, so why did he feel like it was all wrong? The hairs on the back of his neck stood up.

What the hell was bothering him?

He set the boards and toolbox down and put his hands on his hips, surveying the fort. Nothing looked out of place. He scratched the back of his neck and scowled at whatever was bothering him. Eli relied on his instincts, something he'd learned from Charlie when they hunted.

Charlie.

As soon as she popped into his head, he knew whatever it was scratching at him involved her. He ran toward the Bennetts' cabin, heedless of how he appeared. His heart thundered with fear for Charlie. He slammed into Charlie's cabin only to find it empty. His mouth went as dry as dirt. She must have gone hunting without him.

Charlie supported herself with her hunting. There was no reason for her to cease looking for game because she didn't want him with her. Eli knew he was an idiot, but if his behavior caused her harm, he'd never forgive himself.

He turned and headed the woods, to the spot she always entered the trees. No matter if she had her gelding with her, he would find her. Eli would always find her. The ten-minute run seemed to take an hour.

Eli skidded in the heavy leaves and pine needles in the woods but kept his balance by grabbing hold of the trunk of a tree. The bark bit into his hands as he catapulted himself forward. The sound of heavy footsteps echoed from somewhere ahead of him. He picked up speed.

When he spotted a figure coming toward him, he at first could not determine what he was seeing in the dappled sunlit forest. He slowed his steps and anger pushed the fear side.

"You fucking bastard!" Eli gaped at Gunther, who carried Charlie in his arms, the left side of her face a mass of blood. Rage obliterated good sense, and Eli rushed toward them. Gunther stopped, his grip tight on Charlie's inert form.

"You'll hurt her." The big man's voice was deep and guttural.

"Give her to me!" Eli held out his arms, his body vibrating with the need to hurt this monster the way he'd hurt her. "You've no right!"

"I didn't hurt her. She's a good girl." Gunther gently slipped Charlie into Eli's hold.

The weight in Eli's arms was welcome. "If you didn't hurt her, who did?"

"Two blue coats. She got one in the shoulder with her pistol." Gunther looked down into her bloodied face. "She's a fighter."

Eli took a step backward. "How do I know you're telling the truth? I don't even know you." The other man had rarely spoken to anyone at the fort. He had a past with the Chastain sisters and that made him dangerous.

"I never hurt her." Gunther reached his hand toward Charlie and then dropped his arm. "I protect her."

"You need to tell me who hurt her, but for now I need to get her back to the fort so her sister can doctor her." Eli noted the interest in Gunther's face at the mention of Isabelle.

"The angel will fix her." Gunther didn't make much sense, leaving more questions than answers.

Eli had no more time to think about the big man. Charlie needed him. The sight of her bloody, beautiful face made him want to puke. While he wanted to run, he walked back toward the fort trying not to jostle her. Gunther followed them, but Eli did his best to ignore him.

"I've got you, honey," Eli whispered under his breath. "I won't let anyone hurt you again."

He should have been there beside her. No matter what, or how foolishly they argued, he belonged by her side. Mason had been right.

It seemed as though hours passed as he made his way back to the fort while her blood stained his shirt, and she remained unconscious. When he walked through the gate, a few folks stopped to stare, but he ignored them, his pace increasing.

By the time he reached the Bennetts' cabin, he was running. She still hadn't woken up and it scared the hell out of him. He looked back at Gunther. "Find Isabelle."

Not bothering to see if the big man obeyed, Eli pushed the door open to Charlie's small cabin. His breath in his throat, he laid her down on her bed.

"I'm sorry this happened, Charlie. I'll kill whoever hurt you." He poured water from a pitcher into a basin, then rooted around for a clean rag and dipped it in the water. With more care than he thought he had, he cleaned the blood from her face. Her freckles stood out against the pale whiteness. Bruises had already begun to form on her cheek in the shape of a fist. Her lip was split and blood trickled from the wound.

"What did he do to you?" Eli's throat tightened. "My sweet girl."

Her eyes fluttered open. "What the hell did you call me?"

Eli managed a strangled chuckle. He cupped her chin with a shaking hand. It was the first time he felt huge compared to Charlie. She was always so independent and tough. Right about now, she looked anything but.

"My sweet girl." He kissed her forehead, breathing in her familiar scent. "I'm an idiot."

She tried to smile, but she sucked in a pained breath. "I know you're an idiot." She closed her eyes. "What about those fucking bastards who ambushed me? Did you kill them?"

Eli's tenderness vanished. "Who did it? Gunther isn't saying much."

Her eyes flew open. "Gunther stopped them? Not you?"

He grimaced. "I was too late to stop them. I'm sorry for that and for being an idiot. I won't leave your side again."

"I don't—well, for now that isn't important. I told Gunther to go away. He didn't listen." She scowled. "I guess I'll have to thank him."

"Charlie!" Isabelle flew through the door, her medical bag in her hand. "What happened?" Isabelle looked at Eli, panic on her beautiful face.

"I was just about to find out." He got to his feet and stood back so Charlie's sister could tend to her wounds.

"Who punched you?" Isabelle glared at Eli. He threw up his hands in surrender.

"I have never and never will hit her. I love her." Eli hadn't meant to reveal that piece of information while they weren't alone, but it came out anyway.

Charlie's eyes widened. "Eli didn't hurt me. It was two soldiers. A taller, thin one named Volner and a short, fat one. I didn't get his name, but he's the one who punched me. Mad I let him get the drop on me."

The rage that Eli had pushed aside came surging back into his heart. "Fucking Volner."

Isabelle frowned at him, but she didn't chastise him. "I'll let you take care of that. I need to take care of her."

Charlie's gaze found his and Eli fell into her eyes. She was everything to him. Everything. "I'll be back later." He kissed her forehead. "I promise I will always be here for you."

She blinked and he swore her eyes were wet with unshed tears. It was probably just the pain.

Eli left Charlie's cabin with revenge on his mind and white fury in his heart.

Charlie stared at the flickering flame in the lantern until her eyes stung. Isabelle had finally left her alone after fussing for a few hours, nearly force-feeding her soup. Not that Charlie didn't appreciate being cared for, but there came a point when it had to stop.

Her jaw and cheek throbbed in tune with her pulse. She'd refused any laudanum. When Eli returned, she wanted a clear head. He'd said he loved her. *Loved her.* What that meant or how she should react was a mystery. It was the last thing she expected to hear, even if Isabelle had encouraged Charlie to admit she loved Eli.

She still wasn't sure how she felt, but to hear Eli say it so boldly frightened her. After the fight in the woods with the two soldiers, she wasn't prepared to figure out how to reply. She was glad when he'd left, but then worry settled on her heart when she realized he was out there hunting Volner and the other soldier. Eli was strong, but there were two of them.

He was a man of many talents, but was fighting one of them? There wasn't anything he couldn't do if he put his mind to it. Anytime she asked him to help her, he was always there and managed to figure out just what to do. He had always been there for her, no matter how badly she might have treated him.

Soon she was awash in memories of how many times he had been beside her through good times and bad. He was her life partner and she hadn't allowed herself to ever acknowledge it. Without Eli, she would not be who she was. He was family.

He loved her.

Charlie sat up in her bed and wrapped her arms around her knees. Was Isabelle right? Did she love Eli? The darkness of her past had forced her to lock away her emotions. They had been padlocked for so long, she didn't think she could let them out again. Now circumstances pushed her to decide if she was willing to try.

It was hard. So very hard. Facing those two men today made her confront the fact she did need others, the people who cared about her. She was not invincible, nor could she expect to live her life alone. She needed her family and her best friend. She was the one who allowed herself to be alone, keeping everyone at a distance. Including Eli.

When the knock came on her door, she nearly jumped a foot off the bed. It took two attempts to clear her throat. "Who is it?"

"Eli."

"It's about goddamn time." She hopped out of bed, ignoring the fact she only wore a nightgown and that she was lightheaded, and marched to the door. She yanked it open prepared to shout at him, tell him he should have talked to Kenneth about the soldiers, make sure he knew not to put himself into danger again.

The words crowded in her mouth and none could escape. Instead of doing what she intended to do, Charlie threw her arms around his neck and burst into tears for the first time in more than ten years.

Eli froze in place, shocked to his bones not only to have Charlie in his arms willingly, but because she was crying. Not a pretty, feminine weeping. Nope, she sobbed and noisily snuffled snot.

He scooped her into his arms, murmuring, "I reckon I should get used to this."

She cried harder at his weak attempt at humor. He sat down in the rocking chair he'd made for her years go, tucking her beneath his chin. He probably should do something gentlemanly like give her the handkerchief in his pocket, but he couldn't reach it. His shirt would have to suffice for her tears and her nose.

Her warm weight felt perfect in his lap. She conformed to his body as though she were made to be there. The scent of pine and all that was Charlie flooded his senses. She was in obvious pain and he was so very glad she had turned to him.

Later on, he would think about what it meant. For now, he would let her be safe and be herself. He rubbed her back and rocked gently. The lamplight cast the small cabin in a golden glow making things cozy, intimate.

"What h-happened?" she stuttered out.

"I couldn't find them. Fucking sons of bitches. They weren't in the barracks or anywhere else." Eli was frustrated to not find his quarry. He wanted to kill them more than he wanted to avoid prison.

"I w-was worried."

He absorbed that bit of information, his heart performing a weird kick. "Thank you for that. I don't know that anyone other than my Ma worries about me. Or cries when they see me."

"I-I n-never c-cry." She shook from head to toe and Eli tightened his hold on her.

"I realize that. You're stronger than any person I know."

She tried to laugh, but it came out as a wail. "N-not strong. Weak. So w-weak like a baby."

"Not hardly." He pressed his lips to her hair, its curls tickling his cheek.

"Y-you don't know. Y-you c-can't know." She hiccupped and sucked in a shaky breath. She still wept, but the sobs began to subside. "I'm a little girl pretending to be all grown up, but I'm not. I'm not! I want Maman."

The anguish in her voice tore at Eli's heart. He knew she'd lost her parents at the same time, but he didn't know many details. Whatever happened, it was eating her alive from the inside out. His eyes stung while his throat tightened with emotion.

"Whatever it is, you can tell me. I'm always here for you." He continued to rock while she cried quietly. The shoulder of his shirt was soaked with her tears, precious drops of her pain that he wanted to abolish.

"I can't tell anyone or the darkness will come." She spoke into his chest. "I've kept it locked away for so long." Her voice had dropped to a husky whisper, echoing ancient pain into the quiet of the room.

Eli had to convince her to trust him. He had to confide his darkest secret, open his locked door into the darkness he'd hidden away. There was no other way—he loved her.

"Did you know I was from New York? A little town called Brewster.

My dad was a minister. He decided to go west to Oregon and spread the Lord's good work." Eli's chest tightened. "I was old enough to know my father was a two-faced bastard who preached love and forgiveness and beat his wife and son every night."

Charlie grew still. She was listening. He had to keep going.

"I knew how to duck and hide, but sometimes he caught me anyway. When we were on the wagon train, he had to be on his best behavior, but he still managed to break my wrist." Eli resisted the urge to rub the old injury. "Told the rest of the pioneers I had slipped and fallen. Not unbelievable, considering how gangly and clumsy I am."

"You're not either," she mumbled against his shoulder.

He raised one brow. "Then you're blind. It doesn't matter what people thought of me. They barely noticed me because Reverend Sylvester was handsome, smart and charming. The bastard used to cane me if I didn't meet his high standards. He was a bully and I gave in to it every fucking time." Shame raced through him and he was once again a twelve-year-old boy who couldn't stand up for himself.

Charlie raised her head to look at him, her hazel eyes full of concern. Her face was blotchy and wet with tears. She cupped his cheek and he closed his eyes.

"What happened?" she asked.

"We'd reached here one late summer night and he was arranging a Sunday service for the pioneers and the folks at the fort." Eli had to swallow twice before the lump dislodged. "What most didn't know was that he loved women and they loved him. All the time. One of the wives was helping him with his sermon when her husband found them, naked and tangled in each other's arms. The man shot them both dead and then himself."

Charlie sucked in a breath. "Holy hell."

"If there is a hell, he's there. He was an evil man pretending to be a man of God and I'm glad he's dead." Eli hesitated and she sat up straighter.

"Tell me."

"I told the man, Mr. Baumgarner, where they were and what they were doing. I sent my father's killer to murder him." Eli tasted bile as he admitted his crime. "Because of me, he's dead. I buried him in a deep hole and didn't put up a marker. My mother never said anything, but she knew. She knew what I did."

Eli had told the story like he was vomiting up the thorniest, darkest part of his soul. He was responsible for three deaths, including his father's, and he would have to live with that crime for the rest of his life. To his relief, Charlie didn't shrink away and her reaction was one of caring, not disgust.

"Oh Eli, you didn't kill him. People reap what they sow. If he was as goddamn evil as all that, he deserved far worse than being shot." She pulled up the sleeve of her nightgown and wiped her face. "Fucking bastard."

Eli smiled sadly. "He wasn't a pious preacher."

"I'm sorry you didn't have a papa like mine. He was the best that ever was. Papa was smart, patient, loving and had a special nickname for each of his daughters." Charlie's gaze drifted away, full of memories of her father who was obviously a far better man than his own.

"You were chipmunk."

She shook her head. "*Tamia.* I didn't like it when I was little, but it was a special bond between us. Maman loved all her daughters equally, but Papa, he spent more time with me than my sisters. When he died, I was holding his hand. His life slipped away in a breath. When he was gone, I shook him as if I could shake him awake." This time her tears didn't fall, but rather brimmed in her eyes. "I lost both of them in one day."

"I'm sorry." He kissed her forehead. "I'm glad you have your sisters."

"I only had Isabelle then, and when the Beckers took us, I had no one." Her voice grew quiet again and he knew he was close to finding out what was eating her alive. "Camille and Karl were evil, disgusting people. They pretended to be a family, but they weren't. She introduced him as her son." Charlie laughed without humor. "He was her partner in the darkest dregs of life. It's an insult to human beings to call them human. I couldn't stop them, but I damn well tried until…one day I gave in. But before they finished with me, we managed to escape."

Eli knew something had happened to Charlie, but he didn't know it involved a woman and her supposed son. He was horrified, furious. His body must have tightened because she tried to scramble from his lap. He held tight.

"No, you're not running from me." He took hold of her chin and stared into her beautiful eyes. "I love you, Charlotte Marie Chastain. I will never stop. No matter what."

"You can't! You can't love me! I'm damaged inside and out. I won't ever be able to be whole." Her voice shook with self-loathing.

"And you can't tell me what to do. I love you, do you hear me? I love you." He kissed her soft lips. "You, scars and all."

This time her tears flowed freely, but she kissed him back.

Charlie floated between pain and pleasure. Her face ached from the blows she'd received, but Eli's lips were so warm, inviting, softer than she expected. His mouth moved slowly over hers, tasting, touching but not pressing for more.

He held her loosely and she could easily break free. He was Eli, the man she trusted more than any other human being. He loved her. Ridiculous as that was, he'd repeated it. She didn't know whether to punch him or throw up her arms in delight.

She never expected anyone to see beyond her exterior. He didn't know her before she was fifteen and had come west. He knew her as she was today, and he loved her. She didn't have to hide who she was. He loved her *because* of who she was. It was a wonder.

Kenneth was a good man who wanted to court her because she was a tough Western woman. He didn't know her or love her. Eli did, on both counts.

She let herself relax into his kisses. He was pressed against her, hot and hard. Coiled strength under control. He could easily overwhelm her, but he didn't. Instead he cradled her and kissed her as though she would break.

He moved from one side of her mouth to the other, planting the seeds of sensuality. Tingles raced down her skin, raising goose bumps and bringing pleasure. It surprised her, that pleasure. She had experienced nothing like it before. Her ignorance was biased by what she'd been forced to watch. This was nothing like that.

He kissed her jaw, her neck, her ear, sweet, soft touches from his incredibly warm lips. He was careful to avoid her sore cheek and bruised eye. His touch was gentle but insistent.

She wasn't prepared for her body's reaction. Languidness invaded her arms and legs, molten heat followed by intense need. She arched into his mouth, wanting more of what he gave her. She ignored the soreness from her injuries and focused on the new sensations brought by Eli.

"You need to tell me what you like." He stopped and looked in her eyes. His were dark in the lamplight.

"I don't know what I like." She touched his lips with one finger.

"Your kisses I like. I haven't done this before, so we just gotta figure it out."

He smiled slowly. "I can do that."

"Good, because I want more of what you did so far."

He reached for the buttons on her nightgown. She watched as he released each one, planting a kiss on the exposed skin. When he reached her breasts, the cool air washed over them. Charlie didn't wear any girly, frilly underthings. She did wear a chemise and drawers in the winter, but in the warmer months, she skipped the chemise. And she never wore anything under a nightgown.

"Damn, Charlie." His eyes feasted on her nakedness. Charlie resisted the urge to cover herself. This was Eli. He loved her. "I knew you were beautiful all over. So damn beautiful."

At that moment, she felt beautiful for the first time. Eli breathed life into the sleeping woman inside Charlie. She took a deep breath of passion. It was a lovely sensation.

Her nipples budded into hard points as he continued to stare. He reached out one hand and cupped her left breast, then pinched the nipple between fingers. A lightning bolt traveled through her body.

"Holy shit. Do that again."

"Yes, ma'am," he murmured as his mouth closed around the right nipple. She'd died and gone to heaven. Surely no other sensation would be sweeter than this.

He laved, nibbled, suckled and caressed her until she thought she'd lose all her senses except touch. Her pussy throbbed between her legs and pure need echoed from head to toe. She needed more than his touch on her breasts. She grabbed his arm.

"Take off the rest. And yours. Show me more, Eli. I need you."

He moved quickly and had them both stark naked in less than a minute. As they lay on the bed, she watched him, remembering how beautiful he was when she'd first seen him naked a month ago. She should be afraid of this, but she wasn't. She trusted Eli with everything, including her life. He was as beautiful as she remembered. Long limbs covered with lean muscle and honey-colored skin.

"I like to look at you naked." She smiled when his cheeks colored. "You're mighty fine to gaze on, Eli."

"I could say the same thing." He ran his hand down her thigh. "Like an angel in front of me, with a fiery halo."

She patted the bed beside her. "Then join me in the clouds."

His body was so warm against hers. Hot, even. And he was so hard, harder than the trees they used to climb. His hands were long with callused fingers. He touched her calf, caressing and feeling her as though he was memorizing the texture of her flesh. Every small hair on her body stood at attention as tingles raced from head to foot.

Eli made his way up her body with a gentle manner that made her feel cherished. By the time he reached her breasts, his hand had settled between her legs. He parted her folds and she rejoiced in his long fingers as they played her like an instrument, plucking notes of pleasure from deep within her.

He latched onto her breast again and she moaned in delight, "Oh, that's good." Then he nibbled on the turgid peak and she arched into his mouth. Her body wound tighter and tighter, the desire echoing through her like a bell ringing.

He moved to the other breast and she let herself go. The sweet pleasure washed through her, in her, over her. She shouted his name, pulling at his arm and shoulders, needing more. He rose over her, settling between her legs. She opened her eyes and met his gaze. He waited, perhaps for permission to continue.

"I want you," was all she managed to get out, her voice as husky as it had ever been.

He entered her inch by inch, pulling out and then moving forward, a little more each time. By the time he had penetrated her completely, she was writhing with need. This was so much more than a simple physical act. She was freeing herself from the prison she'd existed in. Charlie fought her way out of the cocoon of fear she'd lived in and burst forth into the sweet spring air.

Charlie spread her wings and flew.

When her second release came, Eli kissed her, his tongue twining with hers, dancing, tangling until he'd wrung every lost drop of ecstasy from her body. Only then did he whisper her name into her ear and find his own orgasm, his body hard as steel in her arms.

Charlie could hardly catch her breath. Her world had changed completely. Forever. Irrevocably. She could no longer return to her cocoon.

Later on she would decide whether she was afraid or joyous. For now, she kissed Eli's shoulder and snuggled beside him. While her jaw throbbed from her injury, the rest of her fell into a dreamless sleep, content and satiated in the arms of the man who loved her.

Chapter Nine

Whispers flitted across the fort throughout the morning. Charlie walked to the mercantile with a few pelts she had to sell. She saw three groups of people talking with waving arms and wide eyes just outside her cabin, then another group, and yet another.

She'd been lost in the memory of being intimate with Eli, and her brain was fuzzy until she realized something was afoot. Charlie slowed her pace and tried to pick up some words from the folks who were talking. After scowls and frowns from every person she walked near, her curiosity danced on her shoulders, desperate for information.

No one seemed to want to tell her what was going on, so it was up to her to find out. She changed course and marched toward Kenneth's office. If he was there, he would know what had the fort aflutter. Hopefully it had nothing to do with Indians. There had already been too much blood spilled and her gut told her there would be more. The idea that people were killed because they were different was abhorrent. She had gotten into more than one scuffle with people who disagreed with her.

It was part of the reason the women in the fort generally didn't speak to her. They thought she was trying to be above her station as a mere female. Ridiculous nonsense. She stopped arguing with the fools years ago, but sometimes they got her riled up anyway.

Ignoring the pockets of whispering folks, Charlie pushed the door to the commander's office open and entered without knocking or asking permission. Kenneth stood over a table reviewing a map or some such with six of his officers. The blue coats all looked up at her with mixed expressions of annoyance, interest and surprise.

"Miss Chastain, I hadn't expected to see you today." Kenneth was always so damn polite.

"I need to talk to you." She frowned at the other men. "Alone."

He gestured to the map in front of him. "I'm working at the moment. Can we meet later today?"

"I don't want to wait until later." She would if he said no, but Charlie pushed anyway. They had become close in the last several weeks; at a minimum, they were friends. And friends helped each other when they needed it.

Kenneth pursed his lips. "Ten minutes, men. Use your time wisely."

The officers filed out, some smiling, others scowling—at Charlie. She waited until they closed the door behind them.

"What's going on at the fort?" She dropped the pile of furs on the floor. "No one is talking to me, but they sure as hell are talking. Does this have to do with the map you're gazing at?"

He opened his mouth and closed it again before shaking his head. "You are a force of nature, aren't you?"

Her cheeks heated, much to her dismay. Kenneth had no idea what had happened between her and Eli, nor that her entire world had changed because of it. The brief courtship with this kind, red-haired soldier was over before it had a chance to truly begin. The thought made her sad and embarrassed. She had to tell him. Very, very soon. Just not now.

"Something is happening and I need to know what." She ignored her feelings, which wasn't unusual.

"That's what sent you in here to chase my men out?" He frowned. "What happened to your face? Did someone hurt you?"

She reached up and touched her cheek. It had only been a day, but she'd succeeded in forgetting what had occurred in the woods. "Nothing for you to worry about. I have it under control."

A lie, but she didn't know what Kenneth would do to one of his soldiers, if anything. That told her she didn't trust him as much as she hoped. Gunther had been the one to save her, a fact that galled her. He wouldn't have had to perform such a feat if she'd only been able to take care of herself.

"Who hurt you?" He started to reach out toward her chin, then dropped his hand. "Was it Mr. Sylvester?"

Charlie snorted. "Eli? Never. He'd cut off his right arm before he hurt me."

"I cannot help you if you don't confide in me." Kenneth appeared genuinely concerned about her. She wouldn't, however, tell him anything. She was embarrassed and angry. If anyone meted out punishment to the men who hurt her, it would be Charlie.

"Enough about my face. It wasn't pretty to begin with, so it doesn't really matter." She waved her hand in dismissal. "Now tell me about what is going on at the fort." She waited a moment before speaking again. "Please."

Kenneth blew out a breath, but didn't push her any further about her injuries. "There's been gold found down in the Cherry Creek area."

Gold. The very thing that had sent Mason west so many years earlier. The glittering metal turned men to crazed madmen who would kill for a few ounces.

"Cherry Creek? That's about two hundred miles south of here. Why the fuss at the fort?" She had to admit knowing gold was close, riding distance, sent a tingle down her spine.

"The Army needs to keep the peace, Charlotte, whether that's at the fort or at Cherry Creek." He crossed his arms. "We aren't dispatching troops now, but we may need to. A good portion of my position as captain is to be prepared."

She appreciated that about him. He didn't let surprises happen. Of course, she'd discovered the more she tried to plan for the unexpected, the more things happened she didn't expect. It was foolish to plan to control anything beyond her own person. Kenneth apparently hadn't learned that lesson yet.

"Are you sending some scouts there?" She wanted to be part of this discovery. She'd been looking for something to pull her from her aimless life. This gold rush was it. Her belly tightened, and she knew no matter what Kenneth told her, she was leaving for Cherry Creek. This tied into her plan to go off on her own and get away from the memories that haunted her.

"I can't share all of my plans with you, Charlotte. I have an obligation to the Army." He looked so serious, she had to hide a smile. His auburn mustache turned down at the corners.

"All right, I'll go." She turned to leave when he touched her arm. It wasn't a grab or even firm, but she jumped a foot in the air and yanked the knife from her back. Kenneth held up his hands, eyes wide, still as can be. "Shit, I'm sorry." She put the knife back with shaking hands. He likely thought she was crazy. It bothered her because she genuinely liked him.

"I didn't mean to startle or scare you." Kenneth's tone had changed. He sounded more like a man trying to gentle a fractious animal.

Perhaps that's what she was—an animal. Her world had been torn asunder ten years earlier and she had yet to get all the pieces back together in the right order. She was glued together all wrong and no matter what she did, she could not find where everything fit. Nothing at the fort was right except the time she'd spent in Eli's arms. Hell, the cabin her sister lived in was partially built from the wagon they'd traveled west in.

The wagon of her deepest nightmares, where she was shattered into those uneven pieces.

How could she tell anyone that walking in the door gave her nightmares for a week? She knew it hurt Isabelle when Charlie insisted on living in her own space and she had only relented when it was built directly next to the existing cabin. Truth be told, Charlie hadn't slept well at the fort. Ever.

Now she'd revealed some of the tumult that existed within her heart and soul. Kenneth recognized the wildness in her. The question now was, what would he do about it?

"Sorry if I did the same. I don't like people touching me." Except Eli. He was the one person whose hands brought her peace, much to her surprise.

"I understand that now. I apologize." Kenneth slowly lowered his hands. "If I decide to send a scouting party to Cherry Creek, I will inform you."

Charlie nodded her thanks and left, her throat too tight to speak anymore. She had to escape—and soon—or the pieces of her soul would never come back together.

Eli heard the talk about the gold discovery. He couldn't help but hear. Every time he went anywhere or even when he stayed in one place, it was all anyone talked about. He finished up the repair to the porch outside the officers' quarters and picked up his tools. If he was lucky, Charlie would have supper with him and he could forget about the damn gold discovery.

He'd heard the story from Mason a few times. The professor from North Carolina chased a golden dream west only to end up half-dead on the side of the trail. Nobody but a fool would pursue the fantasy of striking it rich. No doubt many men with stars in their eyes ended up dead in the dirt. Eli pitied anyone that followed the lure of gold.

As he walked toward his cabin, he spotted Charlie emerging from the captain's office. She strode with some pelts in one arm, the other swinging, her head down. She didn't look to the left or right as she marched on. To his delight, she was headed for her cabin. He picked up his pace with a hidden smile.

His mind raced back to last night, when he'd kissed her, held her, tasted her natural passion. She'd been exquisite in his arms. He'd dreamed of touching her again from the second he'd left her. Now perhaps he'd have the chance.

Eli loped toward her only to have a big boot thrust in his path. He headed for the ground, his tools spilling from the canvas bag he held. He landed on his left arm, shouting when something cracked. The same wrist his father had broken when he was a child, still weak from that long-ago injury. His face slammed into the dirt, pebbles scraping his skin like a thousand tiny knives. Dust filled his mouth as he skidded to a stop.

The sound of laughter broke the afternoon air. "You and that crazy female need to leave this fort before I kill both of you, Fixit."

Eli spat out a mouthful of dirt in time to see Volner disappearing around the corner of a building. The sergeant glanced back, and Eli saw a smear of black across the other man's cheek.

That was a gunpowder burn.

White-hot rage slammed through him and he jumped to his feet. His wrist screamed in protest, but he ignored it, grabbed his hammer and took off running after Volner. The bastard had tried to kill Charlie, and who knew what else he had planned to do before Gunther stopped him? It didn't matter if Volner was a soldier and Eli had no legal reason to chase him.

He would kill Volner.

Eli picked up speed, his long legs finally an advantage. The bigger man scooted around the corner of the mercantile, nearly out of the fort through the side gate.

"Sylvester!" The captain's shout barely registered through Eli's anger. "Stop!"

Ignoring the captain, Eli skidded as he chased his quarry. The door was shut and Volner was nowhere in sight.

"Fucking hell." He yanked the door handle, but it didn't budge. Son of a bitch must have put something through the handle on the other side. "Volner, I'll find you. You can't hide."

Eli's wrist throbbed, along with his face. He knew if he went through the main gate of the fort, he'd never catch the sergeant. Aside from that, he didn't have a horse, which wouldn't be saddled anyway. Frustrated and furious, he turned to find Captain Hamilton, his fists on his hips.

"I think you need to tell me what happened to Miss Chastain and why two of my soldiers are missing." The captain was far smarter than the average blue coat.

Eli cupped his injured wrist. "Let's go see Isabelle first. I think I broke something." He would have to trust Hamilton with information.

There wasn't anyone else at the fort in authority he could trust.

Bolts of energy zipped around inside Charlie as she stepped into her cabin. Finally she had made a decision that would allow her to escape the fort. For ten years she'd been trapped by her age, and then her own lack of action. She had been paralyzed by too many outside forces.

Today she made a decision to seize her own path, no longer bound to a place that suffocated her. The act of making a choice had taken a weight off her chest. She could take a deep breath without choking on her unhappiness.

She looked around the cabin and thought about what she would need as a prospector. Warm clothes to be sure, tools, gloves, dried meat since she couldn't count on game. She would bring her weapons and ammunition. Thank goodness she had a gelding, because she couldn't carry everything on her back. However, she would bring only a small part of her belongings. The rest would have to stay behind.

Excited by her future for the first time in a very long time, Charlie began sorting. The pile to take grew on her worktable. She scrutinized her picks and decided to make a traveling case from the pelts she had rather than sell them. Convenient to have animal skins as a hunter.

As she searched for a needle and sinew to create her new bag, a knock came on the door. She stopped midmotion, her hand straying to the knife still strapped to her back.

"Who is it?"

"It's Mason."

She breathed a sigh of relief and opened the door to her brother-in-law. The shaggy-haired former professor had been the big brother she never had, taking care of her as if they were blood relations. He gently touched her face as the captain hadn't.

"I'm so sorry, little one. I can shoot whoever hurt you."

She shook her head. "I shot one of them already."

"Of course you did. How foolish of me to ever doubt that." He smiled. "I came to tell you Eli is currently in Isabelle's care in the treatment room. He appears to have broken his wrist and cut up his face." Mason peered at her while she absorbed the information about Eli.

Her heart thudded and the insane urge to run to him overwhelmed her. She beat it back with effort. "How did he get hurt?"

"He isn't being very forthcoming about what or who hurt him. The new captain accompanied him." Mason raised both brows. "According to my lovely wife, the captain is courting you. I wonder why he is with Eli, then, since that young man has been in love with you since the moment he met you."

Charlie sat down hard and put her face in her hands. "What a mess I've made." She didn't want to hurt either man, not to mention that Jane girl from the bakery, who would be hurt as well.

"It appears so." Mason sat across from her and peered over the top of the pile. "May I ask why half your belongings are on the table?"

"I'm leaving," she blurted before she could keep the words stuffed inside her throat.

"I see. Your sister and Eli don't know, I presume?"

"No, I've just decided today." Charlie wanted to run into her sister's house to see Eli. Worry over his injuries warred with her need to escape from the fort, from her life, from the foolishness her actions had wrought.

"Do you know where you are going? Perhaps to see Francesca or Josephine?"

Her other sisters lived with their families southwest of the fort.

Each had full lives, which pleased Charlie as much as Isabelle's similar situation. Fortunately, only the youngest Chastain was twisted into the knot of an unhappy life.

"No, I'm going somewhere else."

"And you don't want to tell me."

"No, I don't." Charlie could only imagine the lecture Mason would give her. A thirst for gold had been the reason he had come west. Of course, if he hadn't, then he wouldn't have met Isabelle.

"I won't press you for more, little one, but you know you can confide in me." Mason patted her hand. "Now that I've kept you long enough from Elijah's side, I should release you."

Charlie got to her feet and rushed out the door. She was glad Eli was in the treatment room. It was a separate room, like her cabin, built on the opposite side. Patients came to see Isabelle there for doctoring and it was where she cultivated the herb garden she used for medicines.

Charlie slammed into the room and stopped short. Eli had his shirt off again. Her visceral reaction to his naked chest confirmed she wasn't done with her attraction to him. Their one night of passion was only the beginning. For now she had to beat her body's needs back into submission and focus on his injuries. Kenneth stood against the opposite wall, his arms crossed. To her surprise, Jane Flanagan stood beside the captain.

Isabelle was wrapping Eli's left wrist over wooden splints. She glanced at Charlie before returning to her work. "I wondered how long it would take for you to arrive."

Charlie stepped up beside the examining table. Eli's face was bloodied from scrapes and cuts, gravel and dirt caught in the skin. She wanted to hug him, kiss him, hold him.

"Can we go a few days without one of us needing bandages?" Her voice was husky with emotion.

He smiled crookedly. "Good morning, Charlie."

She shook her head. "It sure as hell isn't good." She turned her gaze to Kenneth. "Who did this? A soldier? Is that why you're here?"

"Volner." Eli winced as Isabelle tied off the bandage. "He threatened both of us, tripped me and then escaped out the side gate."

Anger and fear swirled around inside her. "He's back?"

"You should have told me what he did," Kenneth interjected. "It's my job to mete out punishment to my soldiers."

"What did he do?" Jane piped up. "Sergeant Volner makes me want to run the opposite direction. I do my best to stay out of his way."

"Smart girl." Charlie didn't want to like the other woman.

"Sergeant Volner needs to return to the fort so the Army can determine his guilt and, if necessary, his punishment." Kenneth had straightened, his shoulders as tight as a bowstring. He was hiding something. "You should have told me what he did."

"It doesn't matter to you or anyone outside of my family." She couldn't count on help, regardless how much of a gentleman Kenneth was.

"It matters to me and everyone at this fort." He glanced at Jane. "Women need to feel safe here. That's my job. Volner is mine to punish."

"If I see him again, I'm going to fucking kill him." Charlie spoke from her heart. She would never be a victim again. Going out hunting alone was stupid and she paid the price for it. Thank God Gunther had been following her or she might be six feet under, after a painful death at Volner and Oxley's hands.

Jane's face blanched and Kenneth shook his head. Eli nodded.

Charlie didn't look at her sister, not willing to accept judgment.

"Then you would be arrested." Jane was braver than Charlie expected.

"It would be worth it. The man was going to kill me, no doubt after he raped me," she snarled at the smaller woman. "I winged him, and if we're lucky, that wound will slow him down."

Isabelle finally spoke. "What do you mean you winged him?"

"I shot him in the shoulder. At least that's where I think I hit him. My memory is blurry after the punch to my jaw." She resisted the urge to touch her sore face.

If possible, Jane grew paler. "What in the world is happening at this fort?" She turned to Kenneth as if the captain had the answer.

"Things that shouldn't happen to any woman. Ever." Kenneth spoke to Charlie. "I will find him."

It was a threat and a promise. She wanted to tell him to mind his own business, that she would find Volner, but she didn't. She wanted the sergeant dead, but she wanted to escape the fort more.

"If Volner was shot, the ball might still be lodged in his shoulder. Without medical care, his arm could turn septic, or become infected, perhaps even cause hallucinations if it gets bad." Isabelle had started cleaning Eli's cuts on his face.

"Then he could die a painful death? Good." Charlie took Eli's right hand in hers. Isabelle raised her brows but said nothing.

Kenneth offered his arm to Jane. "Miss Flanagan, may I escort you back to your uncle? It seems Mr. Sylvester has all he needs here."

Charlie recognized a goodbye when she heard one. The captain had given up on her. She should have been brave enough to be honest with him. Instead she opted for bravado and loud words. Another crack in the lopsided pieces of her life.

Jane glanced at Eli. "I hope you'll be all right."

Eli tried to smile but winced at the motion. "Thank you, Jane. And I'm sorry. For everything."

She looked at Charlie. "Take care of him. He's a good man." Regal as a queen, Jane tucked her arm into the captain's and they left the treatment room.

"Do you two want to talk about what just happened?" Isabelle focused on her task, but her voice was tight with disapproval.

"No, and it's none of your damn business." She spotted Mason in the doorway. "Now that all of you are here, I have something to tell you. I'm leaving the fort and I'm not coming back."

Shock rippled through Eli at Charlie's pronouncement. Leaving. She was leaving the fort. Forever.

Isabelle's eyes widened before she turned to look at her sister. "Would you care to explain that?"

"I can't stay here any longer. I've got something I need to do." Charlie didn't look at Eli when she spoke. "You have a good life here with Mason and the boys, but it's not my life."

Eli heard an undercurrent in her words, but he still didn't know the full story of everything that happened to the woman he loved. She was a complicated being and he had looked forward to unraveling the puzzle she was made of. Now he might not get the chance.

"Where?" It was the only word he could get out of his throat. It had tightened to the point he could hardly swallow.

Charlie stared down at their joined hands. Her fingers were callused, dirt beneath the nails. Very unladylike, but it was part of who she was and he couldn't imagine her any other way. He didn't love her because she was a delicate, feminine flower. He loved her because of who she was, not what she was.

"South of here."

His heart cracked a little.

Isabelle slammed a fist onto the exam table, startling both of them. "I forbid you from going off on your own to do God knows what. You're not invincible, Charlotte Marie Chastain." The raw emotion echoed in the small room. "You may not gallivant off into the world without a word of where or what."

Charlie's head snapped up. Her jaw tightened, along with her hand on his. "You can't forbid me from a damn thing. I'm twenty-five years old, Iz."

"I will pack my children and my husband and follow you if need be. You will not do this." Isabelle rose to her feet like a beautiful, angry angel. "No force on earth will stop me."

Mason finally spoke. "The gold entices you, doesn't it? It's calling you. I heard about Cherry Creek from plenty of fools with stars in their eyes."

Isabelle's mouth dropped open. "You're going after gold? Are you mad?"

Eli had no idea what Charlie was thinking, but he couldn't let them run roughshod over her. He had to be her knight in shining armor. "Charlie is a grown woman. She talked to me about it but hadn't made up her mind yet. She wanted to tell you sooner, but I told her she should wait. I wanted to convince her that I had to go too."

Three sets of surprised eyes turned toward him. Everyone knew he was lying, but no one would call him on it. Charlie would've left the fort on her own, unprotected, impulsively seeking something only she understood. Eli was used to her antics, but this was the first time she'd decide to leave the fort permanently.

"That's interesting. Certainly an unexpected development." Mason had listened to Eli's confession on who to marry and what to do. The older man wouldn't betray his confidence, but that didn't mean Mason wouldn't spear him with an intense stare, daring Eli to lie again.

"We've been best friends for ten years. Why wouldn't I go with her?" Eli refused to look away from Charlie's face.

"I don't want either of you to leave the fort. This is your home." Isabelle returned to cleaning Eli's cheek.

"No, it's *your* home, not mine. I don't belong here." Charlie stared out the open door, escape evident in her expression.

"Where she goes, I go." Eli hadn't planned to change his entire life, but Charlie was the most important thing in it.

Chapter Ten

The morning dawned cool and clear, a perfect spring day. Charlie stared at the pile of goods bundled in her new traveling bag. The sum of her life was much smaller than she had expected. Granted, the furniture wasn't packed up, but all her clothes were, her tools and hunting gear. She bought a few items at the mercantile for gold prospecting like a shovel, a small pick and a pan. There was another sack with basic food necessities.

Her stomach flipped this way and that. She was leaving the fort for good. Ten years had passed since she arrived here with her sister and Mason. And so much happened in the six months between when she left New York until they settled at the fort. A lifetime of experiences, some good, some bad, some terrifying.

Now she would wipe her slate clean and begin again. It was what her sister Frankie had tried to do when their family left New York. In her case, the past followed her, sinking its teeth into her fresh start. In the end, she discovered the man she loved and settled into a wonderful life.

The same wasn't true for Charlie. Her past lumbered around the fort like a shadow, a hulking brute who reminded her with every glimpse what happened to her. Her past also echoed through the wood from the wagon used to build the cabin her sister lived in.

She could—and she *would*—leave it all behind. There wouldn't be a reason to return except for Isabelle and her family. Charlie could see them at holidays at Frankie's ranch and keep her distance from the fort. It had become the prison that kept her hostage without bars. Leaving would free her and she would finally be able to take a deep breath.

She would be free.

A knock at the door made her jump. She blew out a shaky breath and wiped her clammy hands on her trousers. With a wry grin, she turned to open the door. At least there weren't any dresses in her traveling bag.

Mason stood there, his expression grave. "I wanted to speak with you alone before you left."

Charlie wasn't surprised to see him. Since she'd announced her intention the day before, she knew he would try to talk her out of it. Gold prospecting was a dangerous business, and he knew that more than anyone.

"Come in." She waited while he walked in, examined her belongings and then sat.

"You seem to be ready to embark on the journey of a lifetime."

"I have to leave here, Mason. I can't stay." Charlie wouldn't be dissuaded. "Nothing you say is gonna change my mind."

He sighed and sank into the chair. "I believe I already knew that. I came to ask you to correspond with Isabelle. She's heartbroken right now, but I think with time, and copious amounts of letters, she will get past the hurt."

Charlie winced. "I don't mean to cause her pain."

"I know that, little one. You have your own secrets and we won't ask you to reveal them unless you wish it." Mason was the type of man who was a wonderful husband, father *and* brother-in-law. "Please do not let your guard down while you are out there in the world. Use your fists, knives and other weapons of choice. Let Eli be your hero and your partner. He is a good man, Charlotte."

"He is. The very best." Charlie folded her arms. "He's giving up everything. For me. I've never treated him fair and here he is heading off into unknown danger with a broken wrist." She swallowed the lump in her throat with difficulty. "I don't deserve him."

"You deserve every happiness in the world. Don't ever think otherwise." Mason spoke with an urgency in his tone. "You are one of the most honest, genuine people I know. No matter what happened to you, that was yesterday. Seize your future with both hands."

Charlie wanted to do just that, but she wasn't sure if she was strong enough. Perhaps if she left her past behind, she would be able to.

"I'll try." She picked up her bag. "I need to say goodbye to the boys and Iz."

"I have writing supplies to tuck inside while you're saying your farewells." Mason got to his feet. "Along with several handkerchiefs for tears."

"I'm not goddamn crying." Charlie scowled at him.

"Oh, no, they're for me." He smiled and took her bag. "I plan to weep plentiful tears."

In his silly words, she heard a kernel of truth. Her sister had been lucky enough to fall in love with a hell of a man. They walked together around the side of the smaller structure to the main cabin. The sight of the boys sitting on the step with long faces made her heart pinch.

The three Montgomery boys were similar in many ways—they were smart and mischievous, and each had musical talent. The older two, Andrew and John, had Mason's dark hair and eyes, while little Samuel was the spitting image of Charlie with his frizzy hair and hazel eyes.

"I don't want to see such frowns or I might not give you my goodbye gifts." Charlie put her hands on her hips.

"Gifts?" John—the oldest, at eight—perked up.

"I wouldn't go away without giving you all something to remember me by." She sat down between them and gestured to Mason to put the bag down. "I'm sure your Papa wouldn't want you to be sad either."

Mason shrugged. "They can be sad if they need to. It's a normal human emotion and part of growing up." He ruffled Samuel's hair. "I've purchased plenty of handkerchiefs."

"I don't want you to go." Samuel turned sad eyes on her. "Who else is gonna untangle my hair?"

Charlie didn't want to dwell on the thought of leaving her nephews. It would hurt too much. Instead she reached into her bag and pulled out three small figures she had carved from animal bone over the last winter. She'd planned to give them to the boys for their birthdays, but now seemed a better time.

"I made something for each of you." She unwrapped the dog first. "This is for Samuel since he loves dogs more than anyone."

Samuel smiled and took the figurine with reverence. "I'm going to call him Charlie."

At this, she smiled back. The boys could always pull her from the deepest doldrums. "And now for John." She unwrapped a horse. "The brother who was born riding."

John's eyes widened. "I will keep this forever, Aunt Charlie." He petted the small horse as he tucked it in the crook of his arm.

Andrew sidled up to her, peering into her bag, his face alight with curiosity. "What about me?"

"For you, I made a bear." She handed it to the middle boy. "This is the most special because it was made from the jaw of a bear."

"A real bear?" Andrew had a lisp and was a typical middle child, just like his mother. He sometimes needed more attention than his brothers.

"Yes, a real bear." Charlie enfolded all three of her nephews into a hug, their warm little bodies filling her with regret. It would be some time before she held them again. Her eyes pricked with tears, but she blinked them away, frowning at Mason when he waved a handkerchief at her.

Isabelle stepped out of the cabin, her eyes red-rimmed and her mouth drawn down. "I can't say goodbye to you, Charlotte."

"Then say 'until we see each other again'." Her throat grew tight and she swallowed hard.

Isabelle made a noise of dismay and in seconds Mason had wrapped his arms around her, tucking her beneath his chin. Charlie looked away, unable to accept she was causing others pain. There was too much of her own.

Eli closed the cabin door and took a deep breath. His mother stood outside, her hands tucked into the ever-present apron she wore. She was a tiny brunette with brown eyes topped by slashes of dark eyebrows.

"Are you sure about this?" She had asked him that question at least a hundred times since the day before.

"Yes, Ma, I'm sure." He shifted the pack on his shoulder, the tin plates clanging together. He'd taken all of his belongings he could carry, unsure of when he would return. "I'm a grown man. Sometimes men have to follow their own path."

"I've heard that quite a bit here at the fort by pioneers. You're not going to Oregon, though. You're hunting down something worse." His mother shook her head, her expression disapproving. "Gold turns men into raving, murdering fools."

Eli hid the sigh that escaped. He'd been listening to his mother natter on about prospectors and bad decisions, not to mention her disapproval of him leaving with Charlie. Unmarried.

"You need to marry that girl. Today. If you're to head off into the world, at least you could do it with your wife by your side." Harriet Sylvester was like a badger when she wanted to be. Most times it had to do with food at the dining hall but it also flared up when it came to her son.

"She won't marry me, Ma." Eli hoped one day that would change, but for today, it was the unfortunate truth.

"She's a smart girl. She knows a smart thing when she sees it." His mother headed off, her arms swinging. "I'll talk to her."

Eli ran after her. "You'll not talk to her. She is not someone you can push around." He knew Charlie respected his mother, but they were both strong, opinionated females. Two badgers, in other words. He had no time to clean up after a fight like that.

He jumped in front of her and held up one hand. "Say goodbye here and I'll be on my way."

His mother glared at him, her mouth set in a white line. "This isn't the proper place for goodbyes." Harriet looked around with a grimace. "We're in the middle of the fort. Let's at least go to the Bennetts' cabin."

"I don't think—"

"I won't embarrass you." His mother's expression fell and her eyes sparkled in the morning sun.

"Are you crying?" He could hardly believe his strong mother would be reduced to tears. She was tough as an oak tree, no matter how petite she was.

She blinked hard a few times. "Of course not. We'd best get moving so you can have as much daylight as possible to travel today." With a sniff, she walked around him, her back straight and head up.

Eli sighed and followed. His wrist throbbed in tune with his heartbeat. Isabelle had offered laudanum for the pain, but he'd refused. This journey would be fraught with too many dangers, four-legged and two-legged. He wanted a clear head to protect Charlie and himself.

The idea of marrying Charlie had crossed his mind daily for years. He'd never asked, but he knew now that she would be the only woman he could call wife. He felt guilty about previously courting Jane when his heart was otherwise engaged. Permanently.

They arrived at the Bennetts' cabin within minutes. Charlie sat outside with her nephews on her lap or arm, snuggled up like puppies. They were good boys and they loved their aunt.

She glanced up at him and sorrow shone in her eyes. No doubt she hadn't considered how hard it would be to leave her family. After she and Isabelle had fought to survive and find their other two sisters, Charlie was now voluntarily splitting them up again. This time the stakes were higher because of her nephews.

"Eli!" Samuel jumped up and ran to him with something clutched in his chubby little hands. The youngest had taken a liking to Eli, even had his own set of child-size tools Charlie had made for his birthday. "Look, Aunt Charlie made me a dog."

Eli admired the carving, the exquisite detail she had put into the figurine, even if it was for a four-year-old. "That's a mighty fine dog, Sam."

The boy beamed and soon his brothers were showing their carvings, which Eli also admired. Charlie was gifted with a knife, in more ways than one. A true artist had created these figures. Isabelle was a gifted musician and singer. It would only make sense that Charlie had some level of creativity as well.

Charlie got to her feet and brushed off her trousers. "I traded with the stable master for a gelding for you and some tack. It's time to get moving. We're burning daylight."

"I only ask one thing." His mother stepped up and took Charlie's hands. Eli wanted to groan in dismay.

"Anything, Mrs. Sylvester." Charlie managed a small smile.

"I know you'll take care of each other. You two always have." His mother glanced at him. "Before you leave—"

"Ma, you said you wouldn't embarrass me." He looked to Mason for help, but the older man shook his head.

Harriet, as always, ignored him. His mother was as stubborn as a mule. "Be his partner in everything."

Charlie turned a puzzled gaze at him. He set his bag down and pulled his mother back. "That's enough for now."

"It's not enough." Isabelle moved out of Mason's embrace. "You're correct, Harriet. They do need to be partners in everything."

Eli was horrified. His mother had started something he couldn't stop. Now Isabelle was part of it. Charlie might leave without him if the older two women didn't cease.

"I reckon we should be the ones to decide that." Eli scowled at both of them.

Charlie looked at each of them in turn. "What are you saying?"

"Marry him before you leave. Don't be trapped into pretending like I was and Josephine was. If you're a married couple, you're true partners in everything." Isabelle's voice gained in volume as she spoke.

Charlie stared at her sister for a few moments before turning to him. "Is this what you want?"

From the first day I met you.

"It's a sound plan." He almost winced. How romantic was that? He loved her. She knew that. Yet the marriage proposal was given by her sister.

"I suppose it is. Never thought I'd get married." She crossed her arms. "It would provide both of us some protection."

I love you, Charlie. I'll do more than protect you. I would do anything for you.

He couldn't say what was in his heart. He could only hope she read it in his eyes.

"Will you do it?" His mother's voice was thick with emotion, very unlike her. It appeared letting go of her only son was hard on her. More guilt pierced his gut at the thought.

"Eli?" Charlie stepped toward him. "Should we get married?"

He opened his mouth, but his throat was too tight for words to escape. Instead he nodded and toed the dirt with his boot. Just like that, she turned him back into a gangly teenage fool who tripped over his own feet.

"Mason, would you go find Old Man Jameson? He was a preacher back in Ohio," Isabelle said, sending her husband off to find someone to perform the ceremony.

Just like that, Eli and Charlie were to be married.

Charlie stood beside Eli in a fog. She watched the marriage ceremony from a distance, as though it wasn't her committing herself to a man. Not just any man, though, this was her best friend, the man who loved her, the man she gave her trust to.

Did she love him? She couldn't answer that question and she hoped like hell he didn't ask. The last thing she wanted was to hurt him. He'd been everything to her and in truth, she was glad he was going with her to Cherry Creek. Having someone she trusted at her side was invaluable. Lord knew no one else there would be worth a spit.

Old Man Jameson hadn't shaved in weeks, and might not have bathed either, but he was a nice man. He'd helped a few times when she'd needed to deliver meat to customers and accepted a hunk of venison in payment. The man didn't have a Bible to use, but that didn't matter to anyone present.

Charlie wasn't short, but standing beside Eli made her feel that way. He was so tall and she knew what delights his lean, muscular body held beneath his clothes. The selfish part of her was glad she would be the only one to unwrap that particular present. She didn't want a husband, but she didn't want anyone else to have Eli.

If she were to believe Mason and Isabelle, she *did* love Eli. She knew she loved him as a friend, but was uncertain if she was *in* love with him. There was a distinct difference. She either loved him like she loved her brothers-in-law or like her sisters loved their husbands.

The chasm in her heart told her the former. Charlie was certain Iz hoped it was the latter.

"Charlie?" Eli poked her in the side with his elbow. "You plan on answering the man?"

Everyone was staring at her. It appeared she'd been woolgathering during her own impromptu wedding. Her cheeks heated.

"What was the damn question?"

A few snickers told her that her nephews were amused. Eli reached for her hand and squeezed. Just like that, she lost any embarrassment.

"Will you take this man to be your husband?" Jameson raised both bushy white brows.

This time she was paying attention. "Yes, I will."

"That's more like it." The former preacher grinned. "I now pronounce you man and wife."

Eli cocked his head and one side of his mouth kicked up. "If I kiss you, Mrs. Sylvester, are you gonna punch me?"

A laugh bubbled up her throat and she shook her head. "I reckon a kiss is in order."

He cupped her face and pressed his lips against hers, soft like a spring breeze. She craved more but didn't want the world to see her become a raving madwoman over her husband's touch. Foolish as it was, Charlie looked forward to the wedding night, even if it would be on the trail.

His blue gaze held hers and she saw the love shining from within. He didn't need to say a word to tell her how he felt. Charlie appreciated that more than she could ever say.

"I don't guess you'll let us have a wedding breakfast?" Eli's mother Harriet sounded hopeful.

"We did the marriage ceremony." Charlie wasn't in the mood to celebrate, although she knew her attitude would hurt feelings. She had to leave the fort. Now that the time had drawn near, she found herself nearly vibrating with need to step outside the confines of the fence. "I want to head out."

Eli put his arm around her shoulder. "Thank you, Ma, but we're gonna go. Good thing you decided not to embarrass me."

Harriet laughed. "You're my only boy, Elijah. I want you to be happy."

"I am." He smiled at his mother.

Charlie stepped out of his shelter, eager to be on her way. "Thanks, Mrs. Sylvester."

"I wish you'd stay for a breakfast." Isabelle's voice was thick with emotion. "One more hour won't hurt."

Charlie glanced at the sky. "It's got to be near eight o'clock already." She turned to her sister, hoping Iz saw her need to go. Now.

"I can pack up some food for you to take while you saddle the horses." Harriet hurried away, her small legs carrying her at a surprisingly fast speed.

"I'll go fetch the horses." Eli again grasped what she needed out of the air and took care of it. She sighed in relief.

"Thank you for your services, Mr. Jameson." Mason led the older man away, no doubt to pay him.

The boys stood there with long faces, their figurines in their hands. Charlie knelt down and hugged each of them in turn. "You be good for your maman and papa. And be nice to each other. You brothers are the closest family you will ever have."

"Don't leave, Aunt Charlie." Samuel's tears spilled down his cheeks.

"I will always be here." She tapped their chests. "In your hearts, no matter what. Your maman taught me that."

The boys looked dubious, but she stood up and turned, unable to look at them any longer. That brought her face-to-face with Isabelle. Charlie's own eyes burned, but she refused to cry. She had to remain strong and finish her journey out of this place.

"I can't believe you are leaving." Isabelle's voice wobbled. "And no matter what you say, you aren't coming back, are you?"

Charlie couldn't lie, so she didn't answer the question. She couldn't return to the fort. Ever. She would visit Frankie and Jo, but Isabelle would have to meet her halfway. "Don't forget to keep on with your music and singing. This healer work is taking you away from it."

Isabelle shook her head. "I will miss you every moment of every day, *tamia*."

This was much harder than Charlie expected. She thought she was strong enough to simply pack up and leave. Given how much she shook from an emotional storm before she took a step away from her sister, how could she leave?

The sound of hooves on the hard-packed dirt broke the spell that had surrounded her. She blinked away the unshed tears and saw Eli leading the horses toward her. His mother hurried to catch up to him, a sack clutched in her hands.

Her husband. Her rock. Her best friend.

A tear tickled as it meandered down her cheek. She swiped it away before he saw it. Eli couldn't know she needed him. Charlie was too strong to need much, but she needed him.

Isabelle hugged her from behind. "Carry me with you, *tamia*."

Charlie closed her eyes and tried to remember why she was leaving. It certainly wasn't to tear her heart in two.

"May I be of some service, ladies?" Kenneth's voice cut through her emotional cloud.

Charlie broke her sister's embrace and faced the captain. "I'm glad you're here so I can say goodbye."

"So you are leaving, then?" A glimmer of disappointment slid through his eyes. "I had hoped your sister might change your mind."

Charlie wasn't going to argue the point. No force on earth would make her change her mind about leaving. "Thank you for the company and conversation. I wish you luck here at the fort." She held out her hand.

Kenneth hesitated only a moment before he shook her hand. His hand was softer than Eli's, but he had a firm grip, which she appreciated.

Eli crossed his arms and stared at the both of them, his expression tight. She didn't expect any sort of male posturing over her. The very idea was laughable.

"Mr. Sylvester, are you leaving with Charlotte?" Kenneth matched Eli's expression.

"I am."

"Is that proper?" The captain turned to Isabelle. "Mrs. Bennett, do you approve of this situation?"

Isabelle squeezed Charlie's hand. "I do." The play on words made Charlie snort.

She didn't want to hurt the man. He had been nothing but a gentleman. "Eli and I married not fifteen minutes ago. There's nothing improper about a husband and wife traveling together." She inwardly winced at the stiffening of his shoulders. She hadn't intended to hurt him, but things were what they were. Nothing could change what she'd already decided, what had already been done.

"I see." Kenneth stepped toward Eli, and for one tense moment, she thought there would be fists flying. Instead, the captain saluted him. "My congratulations, sir. She's a woman to be treasured."

"I, uh, thanks." Eli appeared a bit nonplussed. He nodded at the sign of respect.

"Protect her." The captain turned and left. Charlie told herself his retreating back wasn't an insult. He had expressed his desire to marry her. Perhaps it was disappointment, not anger.

"I don't need protecting." She touched the butt of her pistol. "I'll protect you."

Eli shook his head. "We'll protect each other."

Charlie hmphed and took the reins of her gelding. Eli had secured their gear to the saddles already. He took the sack of food from his mother and kissed her cheek.

"Thank you, Ma. Are there biscuits in there? You know how I love 'em." Beneath his words, Charlie heard an undercurrent of sadness. It hadn't occurred to her that her new husband would also be leaving behind his family. A much smaller one than she had. All Eli had was his mother.

"Of course there is." Harriet pulled her son into a hug, awkward considering he had to fold himself in half to reach her. "You make sure you come back, you hear me, Elijah?"

He must have replied, because she patted his back. "Good boy."

Charlie didn't want to feel guilty. He had made his choice and he was a grown man. If he wanted to come back to the fort, she wouldn't stop him. But she wouldn't join him either. She shook off any lingering doubts.

"Are you sure about this?" Isabelle had stepped up, her brows drawn together.

"For the last time, yes. This has nothing to do with you or Mason or the boys." She cleared her throat to dislodge the lump. "I will miss all of you, but I'll see you at Frankie's for Christmas every year. We can plan on that right now."

"Yes, I promise you we'll be there no matter how deep the snow is." Isabelle opened her arms and Charlie fell into them. No matter that she was bigger than her older sister, and a twenty-five-year-old woman, she still felt like a child who needed a hug.

"I will miss you terribly, *tamia*. Every day when the sun rises, I will think of you. The colors of the sunrise are like the beautiful colors of your hair." Isabelle leaned back and cupped Charlie's face. "Write to me when you can."

Charlie nodded. "I love you, Iz."

"I love you too. Please promise me you'll let Eli into your heart." Isabelle's eyes swam with tears.

"Take care of those boys and Mason. You've got a hell of a family." Charlie hugged her sister so hard, she swore a rib cracked. Then she let Isabelle loose and turned away.

It was time to leave her past behind.

Chapter Eleven

Eli and Charlie rode at a brisk pace after they left the fort. He was worried. She had ridden with her back straighter than an oak. Her shoulders seemed unnaturally stiff and then there was the fact she hadn't spoken a word.

Not that his wife was someone who talked for the sake of talking. However, considering their lives had turned around in circles in the last twenty-four hours, *and* they were now married, he expected they would discuss a few things.

She definitely wasn't in the mood to do anything but ride south. The morning heat built until sweat trickled down his skin. His stomach growled, reminding him they hadn't eaten a meal before leaving. Knowing his mother, she had packed three days' worth of food in the sack she'd given him.

His mother's chin had quivered as she smiled at him. He'd never meant to hurt her. Guilt swam through his conscience that no matter his intention, he had caused her pain.

Eli was all she had. After his father died, their congregation had continued west. There was no one else for her. Eli should have asked the captain to look after her. However, Eli had faith that as long as Hamilton stayed at the fort, he would take care of everyone there, including Eli's mother. The captain, regardless if he had wanted to marry Charlie, appeared to be a good man.

As soon as he could, Eli would write to Hamilton and request his help. His mother might not appreciate it, but it would make Eli sleep better, if not alleviate a bit of his guilt. For now, he had to focus on the other woman in his life.

Eli finally spoke. "We need to stop and eat. I've got the food."

"What?" She looked at him as if he'd said he wanted to ride naked. Bareback.

"Food. You know, the tasty bits you put in your mouth that you chew and swallow. Gives you energy and helps you not die." He pointed at his mouth and then his stomach.

She blinked a few times—perhaps her thoughts had been a thousand miles away. "Are you hungry?"

He glanced at the sky. "Got to be midday, Charlie. I haven't eaten since yesterday. My stomach is about to start scratching my spine."

"Oh." She licked her lips. "I'm parched myself. We can stop to eat."

Eli motioned toward a small pond ahead. "The horses can rest a spell and get a drink too."

She let him lead her to the pond and even allowed him to help her down off the gelding. Definitely not herself. He wondered if it had to do with their impromptu wedding or the fact they left her home of ten years. Perhaps it was deeper still, the trauma of leaving her sister.

He laid out a blanket and dug into the sack his mother had given him. Charlie stood with her arms crossed, watching the horses nibble at the sweet grass around the edge of the pond. It was peaceful, quiet.

Too bad Eli wasn't feeling at all peaceful. His gut churned, and if he didn't get some food in there, he might just embarrass himself and puke.

"Charlie."

She appeared not to hear him, her gaze locked in the distance in a place only she inhabited.

Frustrated, he decided to test her patience as she'd done to him. "Should we fuck now or later? I'm thinking now, since we're married."

Her head snapped around. "What the hell did you just say?"

"Oh, you were listening? I thought maybe you forgot I was here." Damn, his words sounded petty. That was the wrong thing to say. What the hell was wrong with him? Stupid, stupid, stupid. He always said the wrong thing around Charlie, tripping over his tongue and rarely saying what he meant. His confession of love was the first time he'd been one hundred percent honest with her.

"Jesus, Eli. I was thinking about my sisters. You turned it into something about you." She scowled at him, her hazel eyes flashing fire. "Fuck you. You can head right back to the fort and forget you married me. That's obviously what you want to do anyway."

Her hands fisted and he had to remind himself she was hurting inside. Her words were always her sharpest weapons.

"No, it's not what I want. I meant what I said yesterday. Where you go, I go. For always." He pulled out some of the food. His heart pounded, but he told himself to stay calm. Getting angry could cause damage to their new marriage, and that was the last thing he wanted. "I still love you, Charlie. That hasn't and won't change."

She took a deep breath, opened her mouth and then seemed to lose all her anger in an instant. As though she were a bubble that popped.

Charlie sat down on the blanket with a thump, her expression unreadable. "What did your mother pack? Isabelle gave me as much as the damn horse could carry."

Eli blew out a relieved breath. "Ham, bread, pickles and what I think is a good portion of a cake, plus biscuits—"

She held up a hand. "Probably cleaned out half the dining hall pantry. I'll take some of the first three."

He put together a plate for each of them, surprised how comfortable he was sharing a meal with her. Their relationship had always run from fun to adventure to anger and back again. He never knew what to expect from her, but that was part of her charm. She was like a package wrapped with thousands of layers—each time he managed to unwrap one, the next one beckoned.

At the bottom of the sack, he found a small velvet pouch. Curious, he pulled it out and something inside crinkled. He opened it to find a paper, yellowed with age.

"What's that?" Charlie spoke around the food in her mouth. She had no artifice, another reason he had fallen for her.

"Dunno yet." He opened the paper and could barely make out the faded writing. "It's addressed to my mother. 'Dear Harriet, I wish you the best on your married life. Your P and I will miss you. Write to us when you can. If you need money for yourself, please sell my mother's ring. She would have wanted you to be safe, no matter what. Love, Mother'."

Eli shook the bag and a gold ring fell into his palm. Charlie looked on with curiosity while he picked up the ring. It had a dark blue stone in it that winked in the sunlight. His mother had an expensive ring tucked away for when she needed money and she gave it to him. Something that had belonged to his great-grandmother.

"It's the same color as your eyes."

He glanced up at Charlie. "What?"

"The stone. The blue is the same color as your eyes." She wiped crumbs off her mouth and nodded at the ring. "Your mother couldn't sell it because it reminded her of you. Maybe why she kept it all this time."

Eli had never seen the ring, but it was apparent his mother had kept it all his life, hidden where his father couldn't have appropriated it for his church and no one could have stolen it. Now she had taken this precious possession, given to her by her own mother, and given it to Eli.

Damned if he didn't feel like crying.

"She loves you very much. That's what mothers do." Charlie's smile was crooked. "Iz told me that even when they're no longer with you, they're in your heart."

Eli nodded. His mother was most definitely in his heart. He knew why she had given him the ring and it wasn't to sell if they needed money. No, she wanted Eli to gift it to his wife, who also resided in his heart.

"Will you accept this as a wedding ring?" The words tumbled from his mouth in a rush.

Her eyes widened. "Me? She gave that ring to you."

This time, it was Eli's turn to smile. "What do you think she wanted me to do with it?" He reached over and took her left hand. "I didn't get a chance to do this part today."

As he slid the ring over her finger, it glided into place as though it had been made for her. A perfect fit.

"Your great-grandma wasn't a small girl." Charlie's voice had become breathy. "Like me."

A breeze ruffled her hair, the curls caressing her cheek. She was a stunning creature, made of all the colors of the sun and moon. His love surged in his heart until it pounded like a drum, urging him.

He cupped her chin and kissed her. She tasted of sweetness and of life. He climbed over the food and deepened the kiss, pressing her into the blanket. Her form molded to his, warm and firm. His body hardened in an instant, eager and ready to consummate their unusual marriage.

Charlie reached between them and unbuttoned his shirt. He smiled against her mouth, pleased to see she was as interested as he was. Her hands crept into his open shirt, caressing, leaving a tingling path on his bare skin. A groan crept up his throat.

"Does that feel good?" She would always say what was on her mind, no matter what.

He levered himself up to look at her freckled face. "Anything you do feels good, honey."

"Oh." She blinked then licked her lips, already reddened by his kisses. Every time he touched Charlie it reminded him of how lucky he was. "Can you show me?"

Although he was somewhat embarrassed, he placed her hand on his nipple. "I like it when you touch me here."

A quick study, she circled the nipple and then pinched it. A bolt of pleasure raced through him. She found the other one and doubled the experience. He shook above her, his body thrumming with need. His pulse echoed through his cock, eager to plunge into her heat.

She pushed at his shoulder. "Lay down on your back."

It was unusual, but everything about their marriage was also. He rolled onto his back, anticipation making him almost giddy. She got up on her knees, her hair wild from the blanket. Passion darkened her hazel eyes. She grinned.

"You're like a table full of my favorite things waiting for me to touch and explore." She ran her hands up and down his chest and stomach, then back again. "You know when I saw you naked the first time, this is what I wanted to do. You are so perfect."

He almost snorted at the thought, but who was he to argue? If she thought he was perfect, then he wouldn't contradict her.

She leaned down and licked his nipple. Her tongue was warm, and when she pulled away, the cool air made his nipple even harder. "I like it when you do that to me, so I thought you'd like it too."

"I do, honey." He could hardly make his mouth work. Need coursed through him, making him teeter on the edge of frantic.

She continued to nibble and lick at his nipples while her hands explored every inch of his upper body. He would lose his mind by the time she was finished. Mad with lust for his wife. Knowing they were married made this experience that much sweeter. He'd never thought it would happen. Everything he'd ever dreamed of had come true.

Her hand meandered down his stomach and onto his cock. His britches were about to burst or they'd cut off the blood to his brain and he'd expire from that. He couldn't stop the moan that exploded from his throat.

She stopped, raising her eyes to his. "Was that wrong?"

"Hell no." His voice had dropped to a gravelly whisper. "It ain't nothing but right."

She continued her exploration, gauging his length through his trousers. Then she unbuttoned them and he was lost. As soon as her fingers touched his bare skin, he clenched his teeth to stop himself from coming in her hand.

"I can't last long. I need you, Charlie." He hoped she took pity on him.

"My drawers are wet already." She would never be anything but flat-out honest with him. "Can I ride you?"

He had to clear his throat three times before he could answer her. "Hell yes."

She jumped to her feet and shucked her clothes. He watched in delight as she revealed her curvy, beautiful body.

"It's a good thing I'm already on my back or would have fainted from the sight of you. God, Charlie, are you really mine?" He blinked at the beauty she revealed.

She smiled as women had at their men for centuries. "And you are mine."

"Come here and ride me, honey." He held out his arms and she took his hands, straddling his body, moving down toward his waiting cock.

She took hold of him and positioned him at the entrance to her pussy. Heat enveloped him as she sank on his length inch by incredible inch. By the time she had taken him deep into her body, Eli ceased thinking at all.

He took hold of her hips and pulled her up, and guided her back down. She found a rhythm and picked up speed. He cupped her breasts, tweaking the nipples. It helped him keep control because he was fast losing it.

"This feels so damn good." Charlie looked like a goddess, flush with pleasure and passion, bringing them both to the ultimate pleasure.

"I can't last. I can't last." He reached between her legs to find the hidden bud in the folds and stroked her. He wouldn't find his release until she did too.

She began to move faster, harder. He held on, his balls tightening and his cock harder than he ever thought possible. As the orgasm ripped through him, her pussy gripped him and she screamed his name. Waves of joy and ecstasy washed through him, pulling into a whirlpool of sensation. He saw stars behind his eyes.

"Holy shit." She collapsed against his chest, her heart thudding against his.

"Definitely." He kissed the top of her head. "Holy shit."

Sweet God, he had married a woman who was as passionate as the sun. He knew there was something burbling beneath the surface, but he never dreamed this. It was more than he expected, and he would enjoy it for the rest of their lives.

The silver of predawn crept across sky, creating shadows around them. Charlie hadn't slept well, not because she was cold or uncomfortable, but because she'd slept with someone for the first time in ten years. The last time she had slept beside anyone was Isabelle in the wagon before they'd arrived at the fort.

Now she had a husband, in every way possible. They'd made love with heat and passion. He showed her how much he loved her with every touch, every caress, every kiss. And of course there was the ring. She stared at her hand, the blue stone sparkling in the dim light.

She didn't know how she felt about the ring or her marriage. Isabelle was convinced Charlie was in love with Eli. Charlie was not convinced. She didn't know if she could fall in love, but if she could, Eli would be the man of choice. He had never showed any hint of how he felt, and then suddenly it was a downpour.

Was it because of Kenneth? Or had Eli developed feelings before the captain came into the fort? Charlie had no answers, and she decided if she asked Eli, it would hurt him more than she was willing to. For now they would continue south and their marriage would ride along with them. For better or for worse.

Something shifted in the small group of trees. Charlie forgot about her tumultuous thoughts and focused on the shadows. Glad they'd dressed before going to sleep, she slipped out from Eli's embrace and pulled the pistol from its holster beside her.

"What do you see?" Eli's whisper didn't surprise her. He'd been hunting by her side for years. His instincts were nearly as honed as hers.

"Not sure yet." She crept forward, keeping her gaze on where she'd seen movement.

Eli joined her, his progress as silent as hers. The horses continued to doze, which meant whatever was nearby wasn't a danger, but Charlie was on her guard. Something or someone was watching them.

They made their way to a small knoll to give them a better view of the other side of the pond. The sun began to paint the sky in shades of pink along the horizon, which revealed her and Eli, but left the shadows in the trees.

"Shit." She started to move again. Eli's hand on her shoulder stopped her progress. "What?"

"If someone is there, they can see us, but we can't see them." He frowned. "We should pack up and leave."

"What?" She swatted his arm. "What if they want to do us harm?"

"Then they'll regret it, since we're armed." He raised one brow. "Mr. and Mrs. Sylvester are a team to be reckoned with. Nobody has chance against both of us."

Charlie had never been part of something like this marriage thing. "Team?"

"It's you and me, for now and for always. You're stuck with me."

She wanted to investigate the shadows and whoever might be watching them, but Eli was right. They were both armed and good shots. It might be an animal or nothing at all. She'd spent so long protecting herself, it became habit. Allowing someone else that privilege would be difficult if not impossible.

"What if it's an animal?" She itched to hold her bow.

"We have too much weight on the horses now. They have to carry us and our gear all the way to Cherry Creek. We can't add on a few hundred pounds of deer." Eli, damn him, was right again. "We can get a rabbit for supper if you've got a hankering for meat."

She looked out at the shadows again. "Even if it's Big Buck?"

He chuckled. "You think that old buck is following us?"

She shrugged. "It's not impossible."

"That cantankerous elk is probably dancing through the woods near the fort now that we're gone." Eli got to his feet and held out his hand. "C'mon, Mrs. Sylvester."

He had been the first person to call her by her married name. Now he'd done it for a third time. It felt awkward, like a coat that was too tight across the arms and too big on the shoulders. She ignored his proffered hand and pushed herself off the ground. She pretended not to notice his fallen expression. Charlie was still hurting him, even if she was his wife. She didn't know how to not hurt others.

"What if it's not an animal?" he mused as they walked toward the horses. "What if it's a person?"

"You made me get up. I was content to pick whoever it is off from my hiding spot." She refused to look at the spot she'd been watching again. He'd already ruined any aspect of surprise she could have had.

"I thought I saw a familiar shadow."

Charlie stopped so fast, dirt sprayed up from her boots. She grabbed his arm, her fingers digging into the solid muscle. "Who?"

"It was a big shadow."

She closed her eyes and let the shudder pass through her before she spoke. "Gunther." Was she never going to be free of her past? Why would that great hulking brute follow her?

"He did save you from Volner and Oxley. That ought to buy him a little forgiveness."

She swallowed down the angry retort. Eli still didn't know everything that had happened to her. She couldn't speak it aloud. She likely never would.

"I don't fucking want him around me and I'm not going to explain it." She started saddling her gelding, her gut churning.

Eli took care of his own mount, the air crackling with silence. Their wedding day was anything but normal. Now the second day of their marriage was worse than the first.

"If we see Gunther, I'll make sure he understands he's not to follow us. No matter what I have to do." Eli's voice had tightened.

Charlie turned to him in surprise. "Are you angry?"

"Damn right. There's something in your past that involves him. No matter how much you try to avoid him, he stays around you. Like some kind of dark angel who won't let you go." Eli's blue eyes flashed. "You're my wife. I will defend and protect you."

At that, she found herself speechless. He finished both horses and made sure their fire was out before they left. As they mounted, Eli tugged his hat down on his forehead. He was menacing in his fury. She had never considered him to have that level of anger inside him. She was very wrong.

After the sweet lovemaking with Charlie, things went to hell quick. She was the one who spotted the shadow behind them. He was certain it was Gunther. The man seemed to have an unnatural need to keep watch on her. She wasn't talking about why. It made Eli want to shake her until she spoke the dark secrets that ate away at her soul.

It wouldn't be that easy and he knew it. Hell, if he tried to force her to do anything, she would kick him in the balls. Or possibly shoot him, then kick him in the balls.

No, there was no use trying to force his wife to do anything. Eli had to use other methods, like earning her trust. He had earned some of it, but not all of it. He knew it and so did she. It was damn slow and that bothered him to no end. He'd had ten years of practice at patience when it came to Charlie Chastain. He would have to put that experience to work or his marriage wouldn't make it.

The fact that Gunther was following them—and Eli was sure now it was the big man they'd seen—infuriated him. Charlie was his to protect. He'd told Gunther that when he appeared with Charlie in his arms. The other man was quiet, but he wasn't dumb. He'd understood Eli, but obviously refused to obey. Damn son of a bitch had followed them. Possibly watched them when they'd made love beneath the sky.

Eli swallowed the rage that threatened. He needed to be in control, to protect his wife, no matter her protests that she didn't need it. He wouldn't let anything happen to her, regardless how many times she put herself in danger.

They rode south, but every so often, Eli looked behind to be sure no one followed. Once or twice, he spotted a wagon or a few men on horseback, all heading different directions. No one going the same way as he and Charlie. Yet he had an itch on the back of his neck he couldn't shake.

"Stop doing that."

"Doing what?" He scratched at the phantom itch.

"Looking behind us. It's annoying. There's no one back there."

Charlie sounded as confident as she always did, but she hadn't once actually checked to see if she was right.

"He's there. I can feel it. For a big man, he's damn stealthy."

She chuckled. "I thought it was my job to do the cussing."

"I can cuss too. It's not yours to own." He sounded childish and he knew it. He couldn't let what Gunther did or was doing turn him into an idiot. "Sorry."

She shrugged. "It's nothing to be sorry for. I'm on edge too, but I can't let it stop us or slow us down. The gold is sliding into other people's pans for every minute we're not there."

He was worried her need to stake a claim would cause disappointment if she wasn't able to. Charlie didn't take no without putting up a fight, verbally or physically. He'd packed as much ammunition as he had or could buy. No doubt he'd need it. Being married to Charlie would be anything but boring or dull. He would constantly be wondering what would happen next.

"It's going to take at least ten days to get there. With this much weight, we can't push the horses any more than that." Eli patted his horse's neck. "They're good animals and we need to take care of them."

She made a face. "Damn. You're right, but I don't want you to be."

"We're lucky there's plenty of creeks and tributaries around to water them. Appears the spring was good for rainfall. The grass is thick, so they won't starve either." Eli had been surprised and pleased to see the land was as plentiful as it was. However, it also meant the trees were thick with leaves, able to hide anyone following them.

He scratched at his neck again.

"Why did you do it?" Her question surprised him.

"Marry you?"

"Yeah, of course. Who would marry me?" She sounded genuinely confused.

"Jesus, Charlie, I told you I loved you. Why else would I marry you?" He was frustrated by her need to pick apart everything good in her life. "You're a beautiful, smart, gifted pain in the ass. The perfect wife."

She burst out laughing. "I *am* a pain in the ass."

"That's what I said."

"You are a saint to marry such a curmudgeon." Beneath her words, he heard doubt, and it made his heart hurt.

"Well, I would've never married Jane no matter what I did. She deserved to be treated better. I was a fool." He regretted what he had started, knowing deep down it was the wrong thing to do. Jane was a good woman. He hoped the captain would look after her.

She snorted. "I'm not gonna disagree with you. I thought you were courting her. Then you married me when I asked."

"I was mad because I loved you but you didn't think of me as anything but someone to hunt with." He shook his head, his gut tight with the feelings he'd been shoving down deep.

"You were mad, so you decided to court Jane?"

"Pretty much."

She was quiet for a minute. "Why didn't you just tell me how you felt?"

"I'm gonna ask myself that question for the next hundred years." He had struggled to accept his feelings and the idea he wasn't worthy of Charlie. "I was Fixit, nothing more than a raggedy poor boy who could fix anything you put in front of him."

She pulled up on her reins and scowled at him. "There isn't a bit of truth in saying you were a raggedy poor boy. Pack of fucking lies."

He smiled. "Yet another reason I love you. Fierce as a wolf protecting her mate."

"If I have to protect you from yourself, then I will." Charlie kneed her horse into motion. "You can be a fool sometimes."

"I already said that." Eli watched her, infinitely glad he'd decided to love the one woman who wouldn't think twice about using the word "fuck". Who needed a sweet, demure girl? Not him.

Movement to his right, at the tree line, caught his attention. He yanked the reins of the gelding and spurred his horse into a full-out gallop. His healing wrist protested how hard he was clutching the reins, but he ignored it. Charlie shouted behind him, but he didn't slow down. Not this time. He'd catch the son of a bitch.

A horse and rider was just visible through the thick leaves of the trees. He pulled the horse hard to the right, into the forest. Eli drew the pistol from its holster. He didn't want to waste a bullet until he had a clear shot.

The rider was indeed Gunther. Eli's fury choked him. Breathing hard, he got close enough to kick at the other man's leg. Gunther grunted and glared at him.

Eli aimed his pistol at Gunther's head. "Stop right there or I'll blow a hole in your head wide enough to spit through."

Apparently choosing his life over his scheme, Gunther nodded and pulled his horse to a stop. Eli waved the pistol. "Put your hands up."

Charlie came riding into the forest with the grace of a hard wind, at one with her horse, her sunset hair streaming behind her. She was exquisite.

She pulled the gelding to a stop with a spray of dirt and leaves. "Elijah Sylvester, you stupid jackass. Are you trying to get yourself killed?"

Eli chose to ignore her. No doubt he would reap the rewards of that decision later. "Why are you following us? Actually, why are you following *her*?"

Gunther blinked, his muddy brown gaze full of misery and pain. "Only wanna help."

"I don't want your help," she spat. "You should have helped me ten years ago. Instead, you let them hold me in that wagon. You could have untied me and let us go, but you didn't. Your mother was a monster and you're a demon from her cursed cunt!" Spittle flew from her mouth and Eli's rage paled in comparison to what burbled beneath his wife's exterior.

"She was my mam." Gunther seemed to shrink into himself. "I didn't do any of the watching or the doings with her. Karl did, and Catherine. I didn't want no part of it."

"That didn't mean you couldn't help me! I needed you when I was a child, not when I'm a woman grown, you fucking bastard!" She pulled a knife from her boot and lunged for Gunther.

Eli dropped his gun and knocked the knife from her hand, tackling her to the ground. The horses whinnied and pulled away, hooves nearly trampling both of them. She fought him like a wildcat, scratching, punching and biting. Eli put every ounce of strength into not hurting her.

"Charlie, stop! It's me, stop!" He was desperate to stop her from self-destructing in a black pit of fear and loathing. She had so much blackness inside her, his heart clenched in fear she would be unable to overcome it. "*Tamia, je t'aime.*" He had asked Mason to teach him how to say "I love you" in French to his little chipmunk. Damn sure didn't think he'd use it like this.

She rolled him onto his back. Tears fell from her eyes, splashing on both of them like warm, salty rivers of pain. "Eli." She dropped her bloodied hands and collapsed atop him, her body shaking so hard, her teeth chattered.

He ran his hands down her back and held her tight. "Oh, *tamia*, I'm sorry. I'm so sorry." His throat tightened for the unrest in her soul, for the horrible things she'd endured and kept inside for too long.

Heavy footsteps sounded beside them. Eli looked up into Gunther's face. Tears ran freely down his cheeks. No matter what Charlie thought, Gunther regretted what had happened to her. His intentions were possibly selfish, to find forgiveness for what he had or hadn't done.

"You can ride with us, but the first sign of trouble, I'll shoot you myself," Eli growled. "I'd like to shoot you now, but I think it would make things worse for her. You're worth less than a rat's fart in the wind to me."

Gunther nodded. "Only wanna help," he repeated.

"Eli," she whispered. "Don't let me go."

He held her tighter. "Never." He would go to the ends of the earth for her. He would die for her. He would kill for her. He would never let her be alone again.

Chapter Twelve

The next ten days passed in an uneasy peace. Gunther had his own supplies, fed himself and rarely spoke. The same was true for Charlie. After her outburst in the forest, she didn't feel much like talking. She'd revealed so much of what had happened to her, shame kept her quiet. Eli hadn't asked her about it and she wasn't about to offer up more information. He might change his mind about leaving her. His face sported bruises and cuts from her outburst.

They hadn't made love since their wedding night. However, they slept beside each other, spooning for comfort and warmth. He didn't treat her differently or act as though she was less than before. Yet she felt different. Her secrets were supposed to stay hidden, not be shouted loud enough to be heard within ten miles.

Yet nothing happened. She almost wished he would ask or say something to her. Instead they traveled steadily south toward Cherry Creek. They started to run into other people in wagons, on mules or on horseback. Charlie watched them with interest. Some watched their group with suspicion, others with curiosity.

She cataloged all their belongings, their abilities and their eyes, looking for the crazy ones. She wasn't about be taken by surprise if she could help it. The more she knew about the other folks prospecting, the better they'd be.

They arrived shortly before noontime to a cacophony of noise, mud and a stench that rivaled any outhouse. They rode past tents, campsites and women tending fires. Everyone watched them pass; most gazes landed on Gunther, the largest of the trio. A good dose of fear and distrust hovered in the air. Having a big man like him wasn't an advantage she had considered, but much to her dismay, she was glad he was with them and not against them.

A few gunshots rang out, accompanied by shouting and general noise up and down the side of the creek. They would have to find a spot where no one had staked a claim before. There were hundreds of people, and finding a virgin spot would be difficult.

"We need to ride up and down to see who's where. Most folks will let us know if we're near their claim." Eli kept one hand on his pistol, the other—the healing one—on the reins.

"This won't be easy." She didn't know what she expected, but it wasn't this. She'd lived in a wagon, camped out under the stars, even slogged through mud. But she'd never been in a place where such a dark presence hovered over everyone and everything. It made her skin crawl.

"These folks will kill you for looking at 'em crosswise." Eli's jaw was tight.

"We stay together. No one goes anywhere alone." Charlie was sure if they kept as a unit, they would be safer. "I am damn glad you insisted on coming with me."

Eli managed a small smile. "I'm damn glad you asked me to marry you."

The ring was heavy on her finger, but it had become a natural extension of her hand. She touched it often, like a talisman that kept her whole and sound. His grandmother's ring had been a wonderful gift from his mother. She hoped no one at Cherry Creek saw it as a nice prize and killed her for it. Charlie was no fool. She knew the darkness that lurked within a human being.

A flash of blue behind a tent caught her eye, but it was gone before she could see what it was. The only colors out here were dirt, shit and gray. Different colors stood out. If she were to hazard a guess, it was Army blue. Her stomach clenched.

"Eli." She spoke loud enough for only him to hear her. "To your right. I saw an Army blue uniform."

Eli's head snapped around and he peered intently. "Are you sure?"

"No, but my gut tells me I'm right." She swallowed. "Do you think Kenneth sent some of the soldiers here?"

"Kenneth, is it?" Eli frowned hard enough his brows almost touched. "I don't think the captain had decided to send troops. And they couldn't have passed us without us noticing. We came the most direct route from the fort."

"Volner." Saying his name aloud sent a shiver down her spine.

"Fuck." Eli tightened his grip on the pistol. "He must've left the fort right after he broke my wrist. No doubt Oxley is with him. Son of a bitch!"

Gunther turned to look at them. "Volner is stupid. I'll kill him for you."

Charlie was surprised to hear Gunther speak and even more surprised to hear him offer to do something for her. "They'll hang you if you kill a soldier."

The big man shrugged. "I ain't got no one else. I promised to protect you."

Disconcerted by the unwanted attention from a man who

represented her dark past, she refused to respond to him. She had tried to pretend he wasn't there during their journey, but he hung on like a dogged cocklebur stuck to her back.

"If Volner is here, he knows we're here." Charlie kept her gaze moving, searching every nook and cranny she could see. "We'll have to be doubly careful."

"There are three of us. We can cover more ground than he can." Eli made sense, but that didn't mean she had to like it.

"It's you and me, Eli. That's all that matters." She wouldn't put their lives in more danger by acting foolishly, but she wouldn't count on Gunther. For anything.

"He'll shoot us in the back if he gets a chance. That man has no conscience." Eli seemed to understand what she was thinking. "No matter how you feel about him, Gunther is here with us and we need him."

She wasn't going to continue that conversation. If there was justice in the world, Volner would kill Gunther instead of her and Eli. It was a dark thought, but she owned it, no matter how it stained her soul.

"Let's get going and try to blend into the folks here so we don't stand out." Charlie needed to move forward and not get stuck in her feelings.

Eli snorted. "There's no way the three of us aren't going to stand out. Me, maybe. You with that beautiful hair and Gunther the size of a mountain? Unlikely you won't be noticed."

"You think my hair is beautiful?" She couldn't help the flutter of feminine pleasure in her heart.

"I think everything about you is beautiful." He sounded as though she should know.

"I'm not even pretty, much less beautiful." The self-recrimination was natural. She couldn't stop the words from escaping.

Eli blinked. "Then you're blind, wife. You're vibrating with life, from your freckles to your frizzy hair. Like the sun, shining bright until everyone around you can't remember their names. Haven't you noticed people stop and stare at you?"

"Of course. It's because I wear trousers and use words like fuck." She refused to believe his story about her stunning beauty. It just wasn't possible.

He pulled his horse to a stop and reached for her hand. "No, honey, that might be part of it, but it's not the real reason. Do you think your parents would have created an ugly child?"

She was nonplussed by his question. "Well, I, ah, no."

"Are all your sisters beautiful?"

"You know they are. I'm the ugly duckling, like in that story." She swallowed the lump in her throat, overcome by the passion in his voice. She wasn't wrong. She couldn't be.

"That's a load of shit. You are as beautiful, if not more so than your sisters."

"Isabelle is by far the—"

"I'm not done. You shine with a light that comes from inside you and outside you. Your hair is even like a beautiful sunset, full of golds, browns and reds. Your eyes are like the spring grass mixed with the colors of that same sunset. You, Charlotte Marie Chastain, are beautiful." He kissed her as softly as a butterfly wing.

She stared at him, unable to muster up another argument.

"Nothing to say?" He smiled.

"No." Her voice was husky with emotion.

"Good. No more talk of being the ugly duckling. You might wear pants, but you're anything but ugly." He let her hand go and straightened.

"Now, let's go stake your claim."

Charlie could barely string two thoughts together. Eli had been a friend for so long, never speaking of how he felt about her. He'd become a different person in the last month. A man who impressed her, confused her, excited her and set her completely sideways. She had always liked Eli, trusted him. Isabelle had assured Charlie there was love, but she hadn't been sure.

Right there, amidst the mud, shit and dirty humanity, Charlie accepted that she loved her husband. It was an odd time, but it was the right time. She loved Eli.

Eli felt like an army of ants had taken up residence on his spine. Marched up and down, as though they were building a structure around his bones that would make him crack like a glass. Cherry Creek was a cesspit. It smelled worse than a stable and an outhouse mixed with putrid food and dead animals.

What the hell were they doing there? This couldn't be what Charlie wanted when they'd left the fort. She'd not shared much other than she wanted to leave Fort Laramie for something better. This sure as hell wasn't better. It reminded him of being on the trail to the Oregon Territory. Only far more dangerous.

Just being there made him want to turn around and head straight back home. He was glad Gunther was with him, no matter that Eli still wanted to shoot the man. The revelations from Charlie's fury made that doubly so. Something was done to her by Gunther's mother, filthy sexual practices that were forced on her. Yet she'd allowed him to make love to her, enjoyed it given her pleasurable cries of release. She was a conundrum who thought herself an ugly duckling.

It baffled him to hear her disparage herself. She had always been so confident all the time. How had she come to think so little of herself? It probably had to do with what happened when she was fifteen, with Gunther's family. Tonight he would press her for more information. He couldn't be married to someone and not know the biggest secret that shaped her life. No matter her bluster, Charlie was wounded and he wanted to be the one to heal her.

They rode through the area, weaving between tents, fires and prospectors with loaded weapons in their hands. They fortunately didn't raise the guns, perhaps because of the size of Gunther, but Eli had no doubt they would shoot anyone who dared to come near their claim.

It was more than two miles downstream before the crowd began to thin. No doubt whatever gold made it this far downstream was less than at the main camp area. They picked a spot at least twenty yards from the closest prospector.

"Check the area. Keep your gun at the ready." Eli gestured to Gunther, who grunted but did as he was bade. The ground was as wet and muddy as every bit of the last camps. Eli found a semidry spot to set up at.

Charlie dismounted and patted her horse's neck. "We'll have to get feed for them. There doesn't seem to be a patch of grass anywhere near here. The damn prospectors trampled this place."

"We need to find out if this belongs to anyone or if we can camp here. I don't want a gun in my face in the middle of the night." Eli nodded to the cluster of tents nearby. "When Gunther gets back, we'll talk to those folks while he guards the horses."

"You think someone would steal them?"

"I think any of them would kill us for a loaf of bread." He hoped she wouldn't decide to shoot anyone before they had a chance to say howdy.

"I don't know what I expected, but it wasn't this." She looked around, her face a mixture of disappointment and anger.

"Greed drives people to do things they wouldn't do otherwise." He knew that firsthand. His father was a prime example of how not to be a human. "Don't worry. We stay together, keep ourselves to ourselves, and we'll be all right."

She made a face. "We need to find gold, Eli. I'm not here to live in the mud without a reward for hard work. Without gold, this would be a joke."

"There may or may not be gold here, Charlie. None of us have experience panning or searching for gold." Eli knew nothing except what he'd heard in rumors at the fort, which was next to nothing.

"Then we find someone who can teach us." She sounded so sure of herself, he almost didn't respond.

"We'll be hard pressed to find someone willing to do that." He gestured with his arm. "They're not living here for nothing either. They want their own gold, their own claim. They ain't gonna help us."

She was quiet for a minute, then she put her fists on her hips. "Then I make them."

"This surely ain't gonna make them like you." He was worried she would get herself killed before he could protect her.

"I don't care if they like me. I'll try being nice, like Iz would be, but I can't fail at this. I just can't." Beneath her tough words, he heard the undercurrent of desperation. It ate at him that she felt desperate. He had to find a way to convince her that life didn't mean she had to always succeed. He'd come to understand what it meant to fail, and it was a bitter pill to swallow, but each time he managed to stand a little straighter. Charlie retreated into her shell like a badger, biting anyone who tried to get close.

It was up to him to get her out of that hole and living her life. Their marriage, and their future, depended on it.

"New prospectors, eh?" An old woman—at least Eli thought she was a female—hobbled toward them. She wore a sheepskin shirt, muddy trousers and a floppy brown hat. Her hair was a mass of silver snarls that had likely not seen a brush for quite some time. Possibly years.

"Yes, ma'am." He tipped his hat in greeting.

"Where you from?" She peered at them with her watery blue eyes, perceptive and intelligent.

"None of your business." Charlie had her hand on the pistol on her hip. "What's it to you?"

The old woman held up her hands. "Just trying to be neighborly." She turned to walk away.

"Wait, ma'am. We're just wary of strangers." He frowned at Charlie. "We appreciate you being neighborly. I'm Eli Sylvester and this is my wife, Charlie."

"She wears trousers," the old woman blurted.

"We know you're not blind," Charlie snarled. "Old women can't be trusted, Eli."

"Nobody can be trusted around here, girl." The old woman cackled. "I like you."

Charlie shook her head. "I can smell crazy on you."

"That's probably shit from my dog, Rusty." The old woman smiled, her brown teeth showing many years of neglect. She might be who she appeared to be, or she could be something far more ominous. Eli had learned not to trust someone's outside appearance. The true test of someone's mettle was on the inside.

"What do we call you?" Eli tried again to find out more information.

"My name is Mercy Rose. Most folks around here just call me Rosie." She eyed their horses. "Fine horseflesh you got there. Wore out, but fine just the same."

"What do you think being neighborly means? 'Cause in my experience, a neighbor doesn't insult, cuss at or interrogate. Not exactly friendly-like." Charlie crossed her arms and widened her stance. "Now you gonna be honest with us or are we never gonna talk again?"

Eli thought about asking her to tuck her straightforward method away for now, then he decided that was the wrong thing to do. Charlie needed to be herself, no matter what. Who was he to tell her to be sneaky or dishonest about how she felt? One of the things he loved about her was her ability to lay out the truth. She was who she was. The prospectors might be dangerous, but together they could keep each other safe.

"I told you I liked you." Rosie cackled again. "We can be friendly. I ain't got nothing to steal, but you do. Folks around these parts would kill you for a full belly if they get hungry enough. You best keep your backs to each other."

For the first time since Rosie had approached them, he felt she was telling the truth. No doubt most people thought her a harmless old woman, but he could see that was far from reality.

"Appreciate the warning. We have one more with us, so there are three." Eli nodded in the direction Gunther had gone. "Our friend is the size of two men."

"I seen him. Wondered if he ate his twin when he was born." More cackling from Rosie. "Big men make big targets. Don't all sleep at once, especially after you start panning. Nothing is as shiny as gold, children. It makes men crazy."

"And women?" Charlie asked. "Does it make them crazy too?"

Rosie cackled one more time, enough to send a shiver up Eli's spine. "Oh no, women don't go crazy. They get cunning. And if you're not careful, you'll be lying in the mud wondering what happened to you."

Charlie couldn't sleep. Their first day at Cherry Creek was not what she expected. The entire place reminded her strongly of the camps Camille had dragged them to so long ago. The smell, the mud, the filthy humanity and the mistrust and avarice. She had wanted to turn around and ride back to Fort Laramie.

Yet she couldn't. She'd left home desperate to get away and start new. Panning for gold held a potential future, one where she wouldn't have to depend on anyone else for survival. She could see right away that this place was not the shiny place she'd needed it to be.

The memories of those awful camps, and what happened in the wagon while they were stopped there, made bile fly up the back of her throat. She swallowed it down and forced herself to appear calm. Inside she was screaming and clawing to flee.

Thank God Eli was there to remind her she wasn't alone. He was the voice in her head and heart that kept her sane and focused. He'd become the partner she didn't know she needed but now couldn't imagine not having. He was polite to the old woman while Charlie wanted to shoo her away. Rosie might have had good intentions, but that was doubtful. She was a cunning old woman who reminded Charlie of Camille.

She squeezed her eyes shut and tried to will away the dark memories that scratched at her brain. Instead the double darkness made things worse. Eli's arm snaked around her middle and he tucked her against him, like an old pair of socks lying comfortable in a drawer.

Just touching him made her feel better. She snuggled tighter until she couldn't tell where she ended and he began.

"Charlie?" he mumbled with sleep in his voice.

"Can't sleep." She didn't want to chat about why and she damn sure hoped he wouldn't ask.

"Sorry." He kissed the crown of her head. "I have an idea that helps me."

"Please don't tell me we're going to talk."

He chuckled against her hair. "No, not talking. Feeling good."

To her surprise, he moved his hand down her body, skimming around her hip. Tingles followed his touch and she focused on what he was doing rather than her own foolish thoughts. He cupped her pussy through her trousers, pressing into her willing flesh. Excitement and pleasure raced through her.

"Someone will see." Her words held no power. She was glad of the blanket around them and the shadows that hid them from prying eyes. Gunther sat ten feet away, his back against a tree, facing the camp. He wouldn't see a thing.

The heel of his hand pressed harder in a circular motion against the bundle of nerves hidden in the folds of her nether lips. Slow movements, sweet sensations she wished she could feel against her flesh.

"I wish we were in a cabin with a fire and some good whiskey. We can take each other's clothes off and spend the night naked, finding new ways to find and give pleasure." Her new husband had become a poet. His words excited her as much as his hand. "I want to make love to you."

She longed to experience what he envisioned and wished they were there already. Sleeping on the cold ground in a muddy blanket was not the ideal honeymoon.

He managed to position his right hand near her breast. He reached through the shirt buttons until he found her already hard nipple. When his hand closed around the aching orb, she had to bite her lip to keep the moan from escaping. Her body pulsed with the magic his hands wrought, playing her like an instrument.

He pinched her nipple, the final bolt of lightning before an orgasm ripped through her. She jerked against him, stars dancing behind her eyes as ecstasy enveloped her, traveled through her and around her. He kissed her neck, sucking and lapping at her skin as she struggled to remain as quiet as possible.

"Better?" he whispered against her ear as he sucked the lobe into his hot mouth.

She let loose a shuddering breath. "Holy fuck, Eli."

He laughed softly. "No, but maybe soon. I need you." His cock was hard against her behind.

"Can I do the same to you? Uh, ease you?" She was glad he couldn't see her hot cheeks, flushed by a release and by a bit of embarrassment.

"No, honey." He kissed her neck again. "Can you sleep now?"

A languidness had crept through her. "Yeah, I can sleep."

He murmured and removed his hand from her shirt. She wished he'd left it there, near her heart, keeping her warm. As she slid into unconsciousness, he whispered, "I love you, Charlie."

I love you too.

Chapter Thirteen

Their first night at Cherry Creek was rough. Charlie wiggled around so much Eli couldn't sleep. He pleasured her for selfish reasons, but then refused her offer to do the same. Stupid man. He could hardly think straight around her.

The sexual release worked on her and she fell into a deep sleep. She even snored. He slipped away at two and relieved Gunther so the big man could get some rest too.

The camp woke early, as the silver light of dawn caressed the horizon. Splashing in the creek, a few dogs barking, low murmurs of conversation. Eli watched everything and everyone. He'd had plenty of opportunity to learn how to observe at the fort. From trappers to soldiers to pioneers, there were all kinds.

Most folks at Cherry Creek were of one sort or another, but alike in one way. They were all mistrustful and motivated to keep to themselves. They barely spoke outside their own small circle of acquaintances. Some had no one but themselves. Those particular people spent their time armed with enough weapons to fell a buffalo and glared at anyone within ten feet of them.

Two women sashayed around at a slow pace, flirting and smiling at the men. Some flirted back while others dismissed them with a flick of their hand. Whores were common around camps. Many times women had no choice but to sell their bodies to survive. After Eli's father died, it was only through luck and the kindness of strangers that his mother found a job working in the kitchen. She might have had to make a terrible choice to feed Eli and herself.

The women made their way close to him. He shook his head with a smile and pointed at Charlie. One of the women turned her back with a dismissive sniff, while the other, a blonde with sad eyes, stared at Charlie for a few moments before she sauntered away. Eli decided to watch those two. Women could be more conniving and ruthless than men, given the opportunity. He'd seen it happen on the wagon train west and at the fort. Fortunately for him, he'd married a woman who didn't have a conniving bone in her body.

A half hour passed while he observed the goings on. A raggedy cat wound its way through the tents, sniffing and exploring. Eli marked its progress in the murky light. As the sun began to slide into the horizon, the cat made it to Gunther. It made a wide circle around the big man, its tail up. Eli wondered what the cat smelled that made it leery.

The feline spotted Eli watching it and stopped midstep, getting into a staring contest with him. Its fur was mangy and matted with mud. It was probably hard for the critter to keep clean in such a disgustingly dirty place. Up close the cat looked like it was less than a year old. Maybe a kitten that had gotten abandoned at the camp and had learned to hunt for its own food amongst the human horde.

He reached into his coat pocket and pulled out a nub of dried beef. The cat's ears went up and it sniffed the air, drawing closer. Eli set his hand on the ground, palm up with the beef in the center. The damn thing probably had fleas and ticks. Why he cared if the critter ate breakfast, he didn't know.

The cat crept closer until it was a couple feet away. It had yellowish green eyes and a mixture of colors in its fur like a patchwork of orange, black and brown. It reminded him a bit of Charlie. Each part was nothing special, but together, it made a unique being. To his surprise the cat delicately picked the meat from his hand and sat back on its haunches to chew. Its gaze held his.

"Picking up strays?" Charlie sat beside him. The cat blinked at her but didn't move, still chewing at its treasure.

"It looked hungry. Besides, poor thing probably doesn't get much kindness around here."

"I expect you're right." She made a clicking sound with her mouth and held out her hand. To his surprise, the cat came right to her, rubbing the side of its head against her outstretched fingers.

"It likes you."

"I'm not likable?" She smiled.

He chuckled. "Depends on the day."

She looked at him with a wry smile. "I expect you're right about that too." The cat rubbed against Charlie's legs and knees, purring loud enough for Eli to hear it.

"Well, I'll be damned." He knew his wife had a soft side, and apparently so did the cat.

"She's a good cat." Charlie petted it for more purring and rubbing. In another minute, Eli would be jealous of the animal.

"She?"

"Definitely not a he. That means she's smart, strong and a good hunter. She couldn't have survived otherwise." Charlie gestured to the sleeping Gunther. "Did you get any rest, uh, before you took watch?"

He loved the fact her freckled cheeks colored as she tried not to mention what he'd done under the blanket. As tough as she was, Charlie was still feminine and sweet. He couldn't tell her that though or she might shoot him.

"I got enough. We need to be on our guard every minute." He looked out at the various tents and prospectors. "Not a one of them would help us if we needed it and most of them would step over our dead bodies to claim our gear."

"I figured that out yesterday."

"What I'm saying is we can't trust anyone. Not Rosie or anyone else who professes to be our friend." He wanted to leave and never come back. He would do what Charlie wanted though, no matter how much he hated this dirty camp.

"Why are you telling me this? I'm the last person who needs to be told to be suspicious." She picked up the cat and it snuggled into her lap as though it belonged there. "I can protect myself."

Eli clenched his jaw. She of all people knew how evil people could be in the name of greed. "We should get started with a fire and breakfast, then see about panning in the river."

She set the cat on the ground, which meowed loudly in protest, and got to her feet. "You're right. We need to get busy." Her expression had hardened. "We're here to make our mark."

Eli knew he'd said something wrong, but he didn't know what nor would he be asking her. Someday their marriage would not be full of unspoken words and screaming silences.

While he set about making the fire, she took the shallow pan she'd brought and headed for the river, followed by the cat. When she squatted to begin, the cat yowled and shoved at her. She pushed the animal away with her hip and did her best to ignore it. No matter what anyone told her, she wouldn't be dissuaded from what she thought was her path.

Eli kept his eye on her as he got coffee boiling and unpacked a few things for breakfast. Rosie sauntered up, the sun behind her. He shaded his eyes and tried to get a read on the old woman's intent.

"Morning, Romeo."

He wondered how the hell this strange old woman knew Shakespeare. "Miss Rosie."

She snorted. "I ain't been called anything so fancy in a long time."

"What do you want?" He felt like he'd asked her that before and didn't get a good answer.

"Nothing, just being neighborly." Her yellowing smile was anything but neighborly.

A commotion by the river caught his attention. Three men had surrounded Charlie.

"Gunther!" Eli shouted to the big man and ran for the river. No doubt Rosie was already helping herself to their gear. She had probably planned it that way, but right now his coffee pot and food stores were nothing if his wife was in danger.

The pistol was in his hand as he ran toward them, bellowing like a bear protecting his mate. The men pushed her into the river and ran at the sight of his face, except one. The smallest of them stood his ground—one hand held a knife too, the other thumb looped around suspenders, a smirk on his dirty face.

He heard Gunther behind him, stomping across the muddy ground like a lumbering beast. Eli had no time to check on him or think of anything except Charlie.

"Are you all right?" he asked Charlie while he kept his gun on the stranger.

"Wet and angry but fine. These fucking idiots decided to see what I had packed in my trousers." She squeezed water out of her hair. "Damn shit is colder than ice. Must be mountain runoff."

The man's brows went up to his hairline. He'd obviously never run into a woman who let every word she wanted fly from her lips.

Eli cocked his gun, never losing sight of the knife in the man's hand. "What in the fucking hell do you think you're doing? No one touches my wife. No one." That white-hot fury he'd gotten under control had surged to life the moment Charlie had been threatened.

"Wife?" The little man had a high voice. "She was supposed to be a man. He told me—well. And you was supposed to like boys." He looked at Eli with horror.

"Now you know I'm not, you little fucker. I should slice your balls off for reaching between my legs," Charlie snarled.

Eli didn't realize he'd pulled the trigger until Gunther almost broke his arm pushing the weapon up. The bullet fired into the air and Eli tried to get control of himself.

"Did you just try to shoot him?" Charlie stared, her mouth open.

"Damn right. I meant what I said, no one touches you. There ain't no call to be grabbing a woman's person." He shook with the need to teach the small man a lesson with his fists. "Who told you Charlie was a man?"

Instead of answering, the stranger questioned them. "Who are you people?" The man scowled at them, as though they were in the wrong.

"Who are you and why the hell did you decide to check to see if my wife had balls?" Eli's voice was tight with the anger that pulsed inside him.

"I, uh, I'm nobody." The man turned to run and Gunther picked him up by his neck. After a moment of struggling, the stranger looked at Eli with sad, pleading eyes.

Holy shit. Man? It was the same blonde whore from earlier, dressed as a man.

What the hell was going on at this camp?

Charlie was mad, but she also strangely calm. Normally she would have exploded with anger if someone dared to act that way toward her. Instead, Eli had taken that role for her. He had done that several times and she was beginning to wonder if their relationship had flipped where he was the crazy one and she was the logical one. That would be something.

"Are you a man or a woman?" Eli spoke to the stranger. As if he could speak. Not likely, considering Gunther was holding him five feet in the air.

Charlie stepped onto the shore and shook off some of the water. "Let him down."

Gunther obeyed, but he kept hold of the back of the man's neck instead while the stranger visibly shook. Eli was red-faced and furious. He'd actually almost shot the man for touching her. Was that a bolt of feminine pleasure? Was she that kind of girl who would be flattered when a man defended her? Apparently she was.

"I'm gonna do what you did to my wife." Eli stepped up and grabbed the man between the legs.

"Well, does he have balls or not?" Charlie wasn't one to wait patiently.

The stranger sagged in Gunther's grip, face contorted in pain.

"He's a man." Eli wiped his hand on his trousers. "Why the hell were you dressed like a woman less than an hour ago?"

"I don't know what you're talking about." The man's voice was husky with fear. "I ain't dressing like a woman."

Eli shook his finger in the smaller man's face. "You're a fucking liar. You saw me and Charlie. Then you came back with two more men and attacked her. And Jesus, I want to put another hole in your head for it."

"And who is 'he'?" Charlie crossed her arms. "You said 'he told me', so who is he?" She had a suspicion but she wanted to hear it anyway.

"I didn't say that." The stranger's voice had dropped to a whisper.

"Gunther, break his neck. I'm done with this fool." Eli turned away.

"No! No!" The stranger screamed and sobbed, struggling to break Gunther's grip. To Charlie's horror, the bigger man wrapped his hands around the other man's neck.

"Gunther, stop." She refused to be party to murder. Being groped in the river wasn't a death sentence.

Gunther sighed but relaxed his grip again. He'd assured them he would do anything they told him to, which apparently included killing someone. She should have expected it of Camille's son. He would never be the type of man she could respect or forgive. Right now the only reason he was there was to be the extra muscle to protect them. Not that he did any good when the three men had her surrounded in the water. He was somewhere else and not watching her back.

She had to be the voice of reason in this trio, which would have been laughable a week ago. Of course, a week ago, she wasn't married to Eli either. Life changed in the blink of an eye.

"Listen, stranger, I won't let them kill you, but you're gonna have to start talking." Charlie realized they'd attracted attention, and that was the last thing she wanted. "Let's go over to the fire so I can dry off and you can start telling me what I want to hear."

"Lady took the horses." Gunther pointed to the now empty campsite.

"Fucking hell." Charlie wanted to punch something. Or someone.

She sprinted for their camp and found that someone had cleaned out all their gear. The only thing left was the mud and a crackling fire. Hell, even the coffee pot was gone. "What lady?" She swiveled to look at Gunther.

"Old lady with yellow teeth."

"Rosie. Damn it." She narrowed her gaze on the stranger. "I was a distraction. You were supposed to make sure Eli and Gunther would come to my rescue. Then while they were busy being knights in shining armor, that old bitch stole every bit of our belongings. Goddamn you all."

They were in Cherry Creek with nothing but the clothes on their backs and the contents of their pockets. And hers were soaking wet. Now she wanted to choke the man.

"Tell me who paid you." She advanced on the man, her hands fisted. "N-nobody."

"You're lying. I know it was Volner." She was desperate enough to reveal her suspicions.

The man's eyes widened a fraction, but it was enough.

"I knew it. That sneaky son of a bitch." She cursed vividly. "What the hell is wrong with that man? Why would he want to bother with us?" She tamped down the panic that threatened. How could they do anything without a horse or food? She had money sewn into trouser pockets, but it wasn't enough to buy three horses or replace their tack. They were stranded with no way to survive and no way to return to the fort.

"He thinks I humiliated him. And he's gone without permission from the Army. If they catch him, he could spend time in prison. Or worse." Eli frowned hard. "He was at the fort the day before we left. I don't know what he was doing there, but he must think we know."

"We don't know anything." She returned to the small man watching them with wide eyes. "You are going to tell us what we need to know." She pulled the knife from the scabbard in her boot. "Or I will personally make you bleed then stake you out for the critters to eat you alive."

The stranger stared at her for a few moments before he opened his mouth. "You folks are crazy."

"And you're not? You dress like a woman and whore, don't you? Why isn't that crazy?" She wasn't judging him, since it wasn't the strangest thing she'd seen. Not even close.

"I gotta eat."

"So do I, and now I can't because your partner stole all my shit." She pressed the blade of the knife against his cheek. "I keep this really sharp, mister. You know why? Because I'm an expert hunter. I know how to dress a kill and cut bone."

"It was Volner!" the man blurted, and Charlie smiled without a speck of humor.

"Keep going." She sat down on a rock by the fire. "Might as well get comfortable while he tells us his story. Start with your name."

The stranger pulled off his hat and long blond hair tumbled out. Charlie could see how he would pass for a pretty woman. Too bad he had to sell his body and his soul to survive. She felt a pinch of sympathy.

"Talk."

"Folks call me Bug. I been here for a month or so. I get beat up a lot so I gotta be good with disguises so I can hide." Bug took a deep breath and let it out slow. "I gotta do what I can for money." His gaunt face spoke of more than a few missed meals.

Charlie didn't want to feel sorry for him. "Get to the part about Volner before the sun sets, would you?"

"A few months ago, he showed up with another man, fat with pale skin and beady eyes. They had money, bought out a couple prospectors and set up the biggest tent on the river. Started paying people to pan for them. They left and then came back just before you got here." Bug glanced at Eli. Charlie now knew where the men had disappeared to after they'd assaulted her. "When he saw you yesterday, he went crazy. Beat up my friend Flora real bad. Said he'd pay anyone twenty dollars to steal your gear. Rosie and me decided to team up."

"And the other two men?" Eli asked.

"We, um, paid them beforehand."

Charlie wouldn't ask what the currency was. "What did Volner say was the reason he wanted our things? He had plenty of money apparently. Where he got it is a mystery."

Bug shook his head. "He didn't have to say why. Twenty dollars is a lot of money. People would sell their mama for that much."

She couldn't disagree. She'd seen greed and desperation and what it turned people into. "Are you and Rosie supposed to meet up?"

Bug didn't reply.

Eli shook the smaller man's shoulder. "Answer her."

"We was gonna meet right after. If I wasn't there, she was gonna take the gear and go, leave the twenty dollars for me." Bug didn't sound very convincing. He was not a good liar, which could help them get their belongings back.

She looked up at Eli. "Where do you think he got the money?"

"If I had to guess, he stole it from the fort. Maybe from the mercantile or more likely from the captain's safe. The Army has money at the fort, secured with the commanding officer. Volner might have known where it was." Eli shook his head. "If that's true, he's a deserter and a thief.

They'll hang him."

"All the more reason to get rid of the people who could identity him." Charlie didn't like the theory, but in her gut, she knew it was the right one. Volner hadn't followed them. They'd stumbled into his dark plot to set himself up as the king of Cherry Creek using the government's money.

"Is there any kind of law around here?" Eli didn't hold out much hope.

"Naw. Volner came in like he was the Army, ordering people around. There ain't been no marshal or nothing." Bug scratched behind his ear. "Mostly it's like a pack of wild dogs. The biggest and meanest wins."

Charlie got to her feet and pulled Eli aside, where Gunther and Bug couldn't hear them. "I refuse to be a victim. That son of a bitch won't intimidate me."

Eli smiled. "Yet another reason I love you."

She felt her cheeks heat. One day she would tell him how she felt, but it wasn't today. She had to focus on getting their things back and not getting killed in the process.

"While I hope Kenneth sends a troop down here like he said he might, we can't count on it." She remembered being helpless in a lawless situation before. This time she wasn't.

"What's your plan? I know you've got one." Eli offered a ghost of a smile. "You always have a plan."

"I say instead of hiding, we look for Volner and Oxley." The idea had started as a flicker in her mind, but it grew in size until the flame burned bright. "It's what we do best. Let's go hunting."

"We need disguises," Bug piped up. Charlie was pleased she'd gotten him to talk. To his credit, Eli stood back and let her work. She had already gotten a great deal of information about Volner and Oxley.

Bug looked miserable and seemed to shrink with each piece of the puzzle he offered up. "All I got is a dress and a hat. Ain't got nothing else."

"You and your partner took all our gear. Now unless you want us to mete out our own justice on thievery, I suggest you help us." She stuck the knife in the ground beside Bug. "Where can we get something else to wear?"

Bug licked his lips. "You got money?"

"Maybe. Ain't much." Eli shrugged. Charlie knew it was hard for him to admit he had little money. It didn't matter to her. "But we can barter."

"Ayup, folks'll barter for stuff." Bug scrambled to his feet, away from Charlie's sharp knife.

"Gunther, you start hunting around for the horses while Charlie and me go with Bug. If you're visible, then Volner won't expect us to be elsewhere. We can surprise him." Eli watched as the big man lumbered off with a nod of his head.

"Good idea." Charlie slid her weapon back in its scabbard. "Now let's go barter some disguises."

He put one hand on her arm. "Let's start right here. You and Bug can swap a few things, and we can swap hats."

"Another good idea. I married a smart man." She pulled off her hat and held it out to him. He did the same and they both donned each other's hat. The effect already made a difference. "If someone is expecting you to wear what you rode in with, especially a hat and jacket, they won't see you as readily in something different."

"Where's the dress you were wearing?" Eli looked at Bug.

Charlie didn't like that particular question. "I'm not wearing a dress.

Not a chance."

"It's too small for me." Eli, damn his logic, didn't smile, for which she was grateful. "Volner won't be expecting you to wear a dress."

"He'll think I'm one of the whores." She looked apologetically at Bug.

"Then he won't pay any attention to you." Eli sounded so sure of himself.

"Why not?" She always garnered attention, since she was usually the loud-mouthed one with a knife.

"Volner doesn't like girl whores," Bug offered.

At first she didn't understand, then she thought through it. Volner liked men, and likely some of the other men did too. After all, Bug couldn't sell his body if no one was buying.

"How long do I have to wear it?" She was not looking forward to her disguise.

"As long as we need to stay hidden. I expect after we find Volner, we can find some way to end this." Eli turned to Bug. "Start spreading the rumor that Volner is a deserter. Oxley too. And that the Army is on their way."

"I thought I was staying with your wife."

"You are, and both of you are going to spread the rumor." Eli took off his jacket, turned it inside out and put it back on.

"That's not much of a disguise." She made a face at him. "*I* have to wear a dress."

Eli shook his head. "It's not a contest, honey. I'm going to smear mud all over me—"

"Not my hat." She liked it too much to ruin it with this thick mud.

"Not the hat, but my face, trousers and shirt. I need to blend in."

He kissed her hard. "Go with Bug and put that dress on."

"Where are we going to meet, and when?" She didn't want to be without him. Funny how she'd wanted to be alone a few weeks ago. Now she couldn't imagine not being with him.

"At Volner's tent in an hour. I'll find it." He narrowed his gaze at Bug. "If anything happens to her, I will find you, no matter what hole you crawl into, and I will kill you."

"Ain't my fault if she gets herself hurt." Bug was more like a weasel, squirming away from any difficult situations.

"Enough. It's time to get moving. The longer we stand here, the more attention we're gonna get." Eli pulled her close for a hug, then turned and walked away.

She wanted to tell him she loved him, to be careful, to kiss him. She did none of that though. Instead she just watched him walk away. Her heart pinched. She shook off the melancholy and straightened her shoulders.

"Let's go, Bug."

Eli did his best to smear himself with mud, including his hair and face. He stumbled around as though he'd been sucking on a bottle of whiskey. He managed to appear drunk and smell like he'd shat his pants. No one paid him any attention other than to try to kick him if he got too close. He spent his time meandering around the camps observing people.

Life had taken a hard right turn for him to end up where he was, doing what he was doing. He was as far from that boy Fixit as he could possibly be. No longer bound by what others thought of him, he was now the man he hoped his mother could be proud of. Now was the time to show the world who he was. He would succeed at defeating Volner.

Beth Williamson

No matter what it took.

After Eli made a circuit of the camp, Rosie was nowhere to be found, unfortunately. The horses weren't either. It was like the old woman took three horses, loaded with gear, and disappeared. Where the hell was she? They wouldn't get far without something to ride, even in the summer when the weather was seasonable. It was two hundred miles back to Fort Laramie. Fort Smith was a little closer, but the Mormons would not help Gentiles. That left them little choice but to find their mounts.

While Charlie could have insisted they pan for gold to make enough money to replace what they lost, she hadn't. Their situation was dire and she must have realized it. Eli didn't want to be separated from her, but if they were to find Volner, they had to do what they had to do.

He made his way toward the largest, loudest tent, suspecting it was Volner's, given Bug's description. Two camp whores fluttered around, but no one was taking them up on their offers. The girls avoided him, which he considered lucky.

Eli had never done anything like this in his life. Leaving his home and marrying the woman he loved had opened up a hidden part of him. One that was fierce, strong and smart. He damn well liked it too. Instead of hiding from Volner or ignoring him as Eli had done in the past, he was hunting the sergeant.

He lay on the ground and proceeded to snore. Loudly. People stepped over or around him, a few stepped *on* him, but he ignored the pain and kept snoring. With a hat down low, no one could see his face. He blended into the scenery.

"Where the hell are they? I offered to pay that goddamn whore to steal their shit. So where are they?" Volner's voice rang out above all others.

Eli told himself to be calm. This was what he'd come to do. He couldn't spoil their plan by letting his anger overtake him. *Breathe in. Breathe out.*

"I don't know." Oxley had a whine in his voice that never seemed to go away. "The old woman disappeared."

"Old crotchety hags can't piss without soiling their drawers. They don't disappear." A bang, and Volner cursed. "Why do I keep you around? You're a fucking idiot."

"I, uh, heard something from one of the whores." Oxley cleared his throat.

"What did you hear?" A slap sounded. "Tell me or I swear I'll rip your goddamn cock off and shove it down your throat."

The man was completely out of control. Eli knew Volner had lost his mind when he threatened to rape and hurt Charlie. Thank God Gunther had stopped him.

"Sh-she said you was a deserter and the Army was coming to get you." The words spilled out of Oxley in a rush.

Silence followed. Eli held his breath, waiting.

"Who? Who said that?"

"I don't know. One of them whores. They all look alike."

"Was it Bug?"

"No, I ain't seen him."

"Fuck!" Volner exploded out of the tent right into Eli's line of sight. He cracked his eyes open to watch. The sergeant stood with his hands on his hips. "Who said I was a deserter? Who?" He grabbed one of the women and shook her like a rag doll.

"No! I don't know nothing." She squirmed to pull from his hands.

He threw her aside and grabbed for the other woman. She darted out of his grasp and ran like a deer. Volner bellowed and turned to Oxley.

"What whore was it?" Volner screamed, veins standing out in his neck and face.

A shadow crossed over Eli, but he lay still, poised to leap to his feet behind the other man and tie his hands. To his horror, before he could do anything, Charlie's voice washed over him.

"It was me, you jackass. I'm ready for you this time. And now everyone can see what you are. A deserter, a thief, an idiot and a piece of shit trash that I need to scrape off my boot."

Eli rolled to his feet to find his wife facing off with Volner, knife in her hand, fury on her face, wearing a dress that showed off her bosom. It was the strangest, scariest sight of his life. He couldn't distract her or it could cost her her life. He had to stand there and do nothing, waiting for the other man to move. Oxley eyed him but skittered away when Eli made a move toward him.

"Slut. Whore. I know what you used to do. I heard you like to suck cock and lick pussy." Volner was mad, completely mad. "I have a big one for you to practice on."

"Ha! I doubt it's bigger than an inchworm." She lifted her knife and widened her stance. "C'mon, big boy, I'm just a woman. Can't you beat me?"

Volner growled and started toward her. Too late, Eli missed Oxley coming up beside her with a gun in his hand. That must be how they'd trapped her in the woods.

"Charlie!" Eli shouted so hard his throat hurt. He tried to get to her, desperately slogging through the mud, his clothes laden with all of the mud he'd smeared on himself. Eli could not, *would not*, lose her now.

Charlie turned and the world slowed down. Eli threw himself

toward Oxley, knowing he was not close enough to stop the bullet from killing her. She would die in front of his eyes.

In a blur of motion, the gun went off, Oxley was on the ground with Gunther on top of him. Charlie jumped back, her face ashen. An unnatural silence followed, only broken by the sound of the river.

"Ox?" Volner stared at the men tangled in a heap. He walked over and dropped to his knees, then pushed the big man off the corporal. It was clear Oxley's neck was broken. A red stain blossomed on Gunther's chest.

Charlie pressed a hand to her mouth and made a sound like a wounded animal. Eli finally got to her side and put his arm around her. She shook so hard, his teeth chattered.

"He died for me," she spoke in a broken whisper.

Gunther had, indeed, given his life for Charlie. He made the ultimate sacrifice in order for her to live. Eli would be forever grateful to him, but for now, he had his wife and Volner to deal with.

Horses sounded nearby, coming in fast, but he couldn't stop to look. Eli stepped back a few steps while Volner knelt in the mud, staring at Oxley's body. The sergeant's expression was utterly blank, as though the other man's death had switched off the mad anger that had been burbling minutes earlier. It was eerie.

"Mr. Sylvester!"

Eli turned his head to find Captain Hamilton and a dozen blue coats riding toward them. It was a relief and a disappointment. He hadn't protected her—Gunther had. The captain had. She had. Eli had lain in the mud and waited.

He wanted to turn back the clock two minutes and get to his feet a few moments sooner. Because of his inaction, Gunther was dead and

Charlie could have died.

"Captain, glad to hear you listened to us. Volner had set up quite a business here in a short time." Eli tried to sound calm, but his voice was raw, as were his emotions.

Volner got to his feet and spat at the captain. "The only way I go back is belly down over a horse. You'll have to fucking kill me, you sniveling coward."

"I'm well within my rights to do so." The captain had his pistol in his hand, but he did not raise it.

"You talk so goddamn fancy. Don't you know the men hate you?" Volner's face was florid with anger and a maniacal shine. Spittle flew from his lips as his voice grew louder with each word. "They fucking hate you! Half of them have already planned on how to kill you."

The other soldiers looked uncomfortable, either at the truth in Volner's words or the fact one of their own had slipped into madness. Nobody said anything, and the silence stretched on until every second was agony.

"Corporal Prescott, please restrain the prisoner." The captain kept his gaze on Volner, seemingly calm. Eli saw how tense Hamilton's muscles were, poised to act if he needed to.

Prescott, an affable man with half his right ear missing, dismounted with a miserable expression. He carried a pair of shackles. "Are you going to fight me?"

"No." Volner grinned. "But I might kill you."

The sergeant moved fast, but Prescott was faster. He got one shackle on before Volner bucked him off. Two more of the soldiers jump in the fray. Charlie started to lunge toward the grappling men, but Eli held her back. He didn't need her to be hurt again.

Finally, four men were able to restrain Volner, shackling his hands and feet. Still he fought, like a worm on a hook. Eli turned and pulled Charlie away. Bug stood behind them, his eyes wide with shock and dismay. Perhaps the little man had more invested with Volner than they imagined. Or maybe he was afraid the soldiers would take him too.

"Do you know where Rosie is?" Eli spoke over the din of the curses and grunts from behind them. "We need our gear back."

Bug blinked and then nodded. "She's out by the shallows, waiting for me."

"Then let's get moving. We don't have anything to do with the soldiers." Eli wanted an end to the day, to the torment of Volner and Oxley.

He just wanted to forget.

Chapter Fourteen

Charlie wanted to puke. The day had gone from bad to worse to a nightmare. And to make things more challenging, Gunther had given his life for hers. He'd died so she could live. She could hardly accept the thought. This man had been part of the darkest part of her life and now he'd given her a gift few would have.

Eli was troubled by something, his jaw taut and his entire body tight as a bowstring. He kept a light touch on her, though, guiding her back through the camp as they followed Bug. The smaller man could be leading them to an ambush. It couldn't be any worse than the rest of the day, including wearing a dress. It smelled, itched and made her tits cold.

They tromped west through an uninhabited scrubby area until they emerged at a small creek. It appeared to be an offshoot of the larger Cherry Creek. The water was a light brown, the midday sun sparkling off the surface. A few small fish darted into sight now and then. It was peaceful, a sharp contrast to the chaos of the mining operations a mere fifty feet away.

The old woman, Rosie, sat at the edge of the water while the horses all grazed on the sweet grass around her. To Charlie's surprise, she was not nearly as old as she expected. She'd washed off the dirt and muck to reveal a woman not much older than Eli's mother Harriet. Rosie was hiding in plain sight.

"Is your name even Rosie?" Charlie sat down, her legs still shaky from the violence.

"It's whatever I want it to be. Today, Rosie." She smiled, revealing teeth that had also been scrubbed free from the yellowish stains. Charlie was startled to discover Rosie was almost pretty. Her ability to hide her true nature was impressive. "What happened to Volner?" She spoke to Bug, who had flopped down beside her.

"Army came and took him. It was the damnedest thing I've ever seen." Bug shook his head. "The big man cracked Oxley's neck."

"Well then, the game changes again." Rosie twirled a piece of grass in her fingers. "The field is open for someone else to make a run at being a boss."

Charlie had the impression that person would be Rosie. "We're taking our gear and the horses. You and Bug helped us when you could have left us with nothing." She didn't want to forget what they'd done, good or bad. Perhaps, though, Gunther's sacrifice would give these two wayward souls a chance to start over. "If you want it, you can have Gunther's horse."

"Fair enough. He'll fetch a good price if we sell him." Rosie was far more cunning than any of the men at the camp. At that moment, she reminded Charlie of Camille, which sent a shiver of dread down her spine. "I mean you no harm, you or your man. I was just protecting Bug."

Charlie stared at the two of them. "He's your son?"

A flash of pain moved through the older woman's expression. "Most folks don't see that."

"He has your eyes." Charlie wrapped her arms around her knees. "I understand about mothers protecting their children."

"I've done what I did to survive. I tried to keep him safe, but the world can be cruel." Rosie took Bug's hand and squeezed it. "We take care of each other now."

Charlie's discomfort began to fade. Perhaps Rosie wasn't really like Camille. She seemed genuine, but she'd also seemed genuine when she was acting like a crone. Trusting people was tricky business.

Eli had watched without speaking for a few minutes. "My mother did what she had to. We would have starved or died that first winter if she hadn't gotten a job at the fort." He had experiences unlike Charlie's and was very close to Harriet. The parallel between the mothers was unmistakable.

What would her mother have done to protect Charlie or her sisters? Anything, including giving her life, which in the end, she did. An ache began in Charlie's heart and she missed Maman so hard, her eyes pricked with tears. She buried her face in her arms and swallowed several times.

A light touch on her hand made her raise her head. Rosie looked at her with sympathy. "Thank you for not revealing Bug to everyone. He is everything to me."

Eli tipped Charlie's chin up until she met his gaze. "Ah, *tamia, je t'aime.*" It was awkward French and she could tell he'd been practicing. Isabelle or Mason probably taught him. For her.

She launched herself into arms and allowed herself to cry. Tears she had been holding in escaped. Charlie allowed herself to weep for the child she was, the parents she lost, the life she lost, and the woman who hadn't allowed herself to grieve. Eli held her tight, quiet and strong.

Eli wet his handkerchief and wiped Charlie's face. Her eyes were swollen and her nose was red. She allowed him to minister to her. Soon she would take back control of herself, but for now she was complacent. The weeping had bothered him to his core. He'd rarely seen her cry, and he knew she didn't allow herself to let tears flow easily.

Somehow the damn cat found them and wound its way around Charlie, settling in her lap. The mangy feline hissed at him when he tried to move it.

"You want some water?" He grabbed the canteen from the saddle resting on a rock nearby.

Rosie and Bug had retreated about twenty feet away and were talking quietly to each other. They had given Charlie privacy to get hold of her emotions and Eli was grateful for it. She sipped at the water and eyed him.

"You smell."

He blinked and then smiled, pleased to see her spark back. "I was in disguise."

"So am I. I need to get this damn dress off." She swiped at her hair and tugged at the hat on his head. "Give me my hat back."

He handed her the hat. "Where's mine?" He didn't really care about the old thing, but it was something to distract her.

"Back there. Trampled in the fight." She shrugged. "I'm sorry about what I just did." She fiddled with the brim of the hat.

He took her hand and kissed it. "I'm not. Your body tells you what you need. You finally listened to it."

"Are you going to wash up? 'Cause you're making my eyes water." She would probably never want to talk about her feelings, but at least she wasn't angry about crying.

"Don't want to offend your ladyship." He got to his feet and took off his jacket, which was heavy with mud. It could almost stand up on its own. He pulled off his shirt and Charlie sat up straighter.

"Every time I see you without a shirt, I want to touch you."

His body flushed with heat. They weren't alone and they were in a place anyone could see them. Still, he wanted to capture the passion in her eyes and lose himself in her body. The air between them crackled with sexual need. It had been almost two weeks since they made love. He wanted her. Here. Now.

"You'd best get that mud out of your clothes, Mr. Sylvester. That mud is caked with shit. Your trousers ain't ever gonna smell right if you don't get 'em clean now." Rosie had approached, her back no longer stooped. She really was a master of disguise.

Eli shifted out of view so the older woman wouldn't see the steel rod in his britches. He slipped off his boots and headed for the water. While the small creek wasn't crystal clear, it would get the worst of the mud off. He waded into the foot deep water with his shirt in hand. He got to his knees and used the sand under his feet to scrub the mud away.

Charlie stood. "Where are my trousers, Bug? I am done wearing this frippery."

Bug grinned and pulled her clothes from a bag near the horses. "You didn't get my dress dirty, did you?"

"Fortunately I didn't piss my drawers." She returned the grin, the sun shining on her unbound hair, turning it into an explosion of color. Eli couldn't imagine a more beautiful sight. "No peeking while I change or I'll pound you."

Bug turned his back and stared off into the distance. Charlie looked at Eli as she pulled the dress off. Her exquisite body called to him and his erection raged and howled. As soon as they found some privacy he would taste the treat his wife offered, again and again.

To his disappointment, she pulled on her shirt and trousers, followed by her boots. "Thank God. I was starting to feel like a damn girl." Eli laughed and she sauntered over to him. "You're looking mighty shiny in that creek."

"You can join me."

Her gaze followed the water as it ran down his chest. "You make a tempting offer." Her expression changed the longer she stared at him. She drew closer, now frowning fiercely. "Eli, you're shiny."

"You said that. Is that a bad thing?" He squeezed the water from his shirt.

Charlie ran toward him, slogging through the water, her hands outstretched. He didn't know what the hell she was doing, but after she realized her boots were full of creek water, she would be mighty angry.

"You're shiny." She ran her hands down his chest and held it out to him. "I mean really shiny!"

He looked at her hand and finally saw what she did. Gold. He was covered in tiny flecks of gold. While the other miners were panning the main creek, the smaller one held concentrated amounts.

"Holy shit." He shook his head. "Does this mean we make a claim here?" He didn't know if she really wanted to be there, but now that there was real gold involved, she might.

Charlie ran her finger through the flecks on her palm. "We could be rich if we did."

"Yes, we could. It would be a lot of work, and dangerous. Those people would slit our throats for a good claim if they could." She touched his chest, splaying her fingers on his flesh. He wanted her to do more than touch him to gather gold. "Is that what you want?"

She ran her hands down his arms and looked into his eyes, their hazel depths more beautiful than any gold. "Why did you marry me?"

At first he couldn't reply, his mind trying to follow the abrupt change in subject. "I love you. I've wanted to marry you since the moment I met you."

"I'm damaged, Eli. I can't ever be whole."

He cupped her face and kissed her plump lips. "You are the woman I love. I don't know who you were before. I only know you now. You're whole to me."

"They did things to me. Forced me to do things to Karl while she watched. I tried to fight them, but he was too strong." Her eyes shimmered with dark emotion. "I wanted to die."

Agony for all she'd suffered nearly made him weep. "I wish I could kill them for you."

"They are all dead. And now Gunther. He didn't do anything but what his mother told him to. He never watched or was part of it, but he did nothing to stop it. I hated him." Her chin trembled. "I hated him for doing nothing as much as I hated myself for letting it happen."

"You were a child, a girl who was held hostage. There's no blame at your feet." He ran his thumbs across her cheeks.

"I had no one else to blame. It's a wound deep inside me that won't heal. I'm broken," she repeated. "I'm sorry I pushed you to marry me."

He kissed her forehead. "I'm not. We're a team, remember? Where you go, I go. No matter where that is."

She wrapped her arms around him and he held her tight. Tighter than ever. "I love you, Eli."

His heart sang at the four words she'd murmured against his shoulder. He'd never thought to hear them, but he'd damn well hoped to. He kissed the side of her head. "Honey, I love you too. More than you will ever know."

They stood there for several minutes, not speaking with words, but with their hearts. Neither of them would be perfect and they would no doubt fight and struggle at times, but they would also make love, find happiness and grow old at each other's side. No matter where they chose to live.

"You two want to be alone?" Rosie stood with her hands on her hips, frowning.

Eli looked at Charlie. "You choose. I go where you go."

"I want to go home, but before that I want to see Frankie and Jo." To his relief, she smiled and kissed him. "We go together. For now and for always."

Eli smiled. "Rosie, you and Bug need to stake a claim. I think we found your gold. Charlie and I are going home."

The day was still young when they left Cherry Creek. The journey there, the discovery and the experience had felt like a lifetime and not merely two weeks. She was emotionally drained, but at the same time, more at peace than she had been since she left New York so many years ago.

Facing what had happened to her had been painful, but afterwards, she had finally cried, releasing the demons that had taken up residence in her heart. Now they were gone, leaving her exhausted but free. Eli had been at her side for ten years and she hadn't seen him, not until she saw him naked. Then her world had changed, turning again when he had told her how he felt.

She truly had been living in a cocoon of anger and agony, unwilling to come out. Eli had showed her what it meant to live. Gunther had taught her that everyone can be forgiven. He'd protected her no matter how often she expressed her hatred for him. He might have been a simple man, but he saved her life and in turn gave his own.

Charlie didn't understand why, but perhaps she didn't need to. Everyone had their own personal demons to exorcise. Gunther's might have been what he did for his mother or what he didn't do because of her. It was his struggle to overcome. Charlie hoped he found peace too and would rest easy knowing she had forgiven him.

To her surprise, granting that forgiveness had lifted a weight off her chest, one she hadn't realized was there until it was gone. Eli's acceptance of her as she was also lightened her heart and soul. She was going to be all right. Her life would be spent with the man who helped her be whole again.

She might not ever sing or skip like she used to, but Charlie knew she would be less angry and afraid. Eli had given her the gift of his love. The wedding ring on her finger was now part of her soul and her heart. Life could not be any better.

They were headed to Frankie's house. Charlie had a few things to tell both her eldest sister and Jo, who lived near Frankie. She had avoided the two of them for years, only visiting at Christmas, and not every year. She owed them an apology and an explanation. Charlie was confident she would be able to finally tell them what happened to her.

After that, she and Eli would go home. Strange how she'd wanted to leave the fort since the moment she'd arrived and now she couldn't wait to return. It was home, where she met Eli, where she grew into an adult, and where they would live. Perhaps one day they might move to someplace new, but that wouldn't be now.

Charlie was lost in thought, her attention on the trail ahead. When the gunshot sounded, it took her a moment to recognize what it was. She turned behind her to see Volner riding at them hell for leather, a pistol pointed at her head. Dread seized her for a split second, but she was ready for the second shot. She jerked her horse to the right, and a searing pain burned across her cheek.

Charlie thought for certain Volner would kill both of them. How had the man escaped from Kenneth and the soldiers? She didn't want to think the nice captain had been killed or injured. The sergeant should've been hung as a deserter on the spot at Cherry Creek. She knew better than most what happened when a rabid dog wasn't put down when it showed signs of madness.

Before she could get her pistol from its holster, Eli turned around in his saddle, gun in hand, aimed and fired. Volner screamed and slumped sideways, falling off the saddle. Charlie pulled her gelding to a stop, her heart beating hard enough to make her ears hurt. Her husband turned back around, then pulled his horse back around toward her. His brows were slammed together in an angry V.

"He shot you. Fuck." He reached her in seconds, his face flushed and lips in a white line.

"He shot me?" She touched her stinging cheek, surprised to see blood on her fingers.

"There's a goddamn furrow in your cheek. Took off a few freckles and a strip of skin." He pulled his handkerchief again and pressed it to her cheek. "I'm sorry, honey."

She shook her head. "Sorry? I don't know why. How could anyone ever mistake you for a man who's only good at fixing things? You're a fucking cowboy, Eli." She pulled him toward her and kissed him with all the passion and love in her heart. "You saved me."

"I reckon I did." His expression relaxed a little. "I didn't think of anything but killing him before he killed you."

"You saved me," she repeated, then kissed him again. "Thank you."

"You won't thank me when you see the scar. I should have shot him before he was able to get that second shot off."

"Doesn't matter. I have scars inside and out. One more won't make a difference, even if stings like a bitch." She took the handkerchief and held it to the wound. "You should check to be sure if he's dead."

He frowned but nodded and turned his horse around to ride toward where Volner fell. The birds sang and bees buzzed around her. Nature continued reminding her life didn't stop even if she wanted it to. Eli reached the fallen madman and looked down intently for a few moments. He returned to her with a grim expression.

"He's dead. Blew the back of his head clean off. And I sure as hell don't feel guilty."

"You shouldn't. He was a bastard who had caused a great deal of harm to other people. You reap what you sow." She refused to feel guilty for being glad Volner was dead.

"Do we leave him here?" Eli glanced around. "I expect scavengers would get to him."

No matter how much she hated Volner, she didn't want to leave his body for coyotes and vultures. It was the lady in her. Her mother would be proud Charlie had learned a few things from her.

"I suppose we can load his body on the horse he was riding." Before she could wonder aloud where Kenneth was, the soldiers were riding toward them in two columns, the redheaded captain at the lead.

Eli held up his hands, palms out, and then pointed at the ground where Volner was. The soldiers pulled their mounts in a circle around the body. Kenneth rode to Eli and Charlie, his face a mass of cuts, with a black eye.

"What happened?" She was surprised to see the man who was always in control so flustered.

"Volner got free and escaped." That was apparently all Kenneth was going to say about it. "He shot you?"

"A graze." She dabbed at her cheek and winced. "Nothing serious, and I have a few remedies in my bag to treat it later."

"Good to hear. You shot him?"

She shook her head. "No, Eli did. Damnedest thing I ever saw. He spun around in the saddle and hit Volner at a dead run."

The captain's brows went up toward his hairline. "Well, then, thank you for your service to the Army, Mr. Sylvester. I'm glad to see Charlotte has a husband who can take care of her."

Eli frowned at the backhanded compliment. "There was never any doubt I would."

Kenneth ignored the remark, which might have been a good thing. The last thing the captain needed was another fight, although a little feminine part of her preened a bit over the male posturing. "My troop and I will see to his body. He killed another of the soldiers in his escape. We're going to bury both of them and be on our way back to Fort Laramie. If you've a mind to have an escort, you can wait an hour for us to do our duty."

Charlie looked at Eli and saw the need in his eyes, one she was sure was echoed in her own. "We're headed west to my sister Frankie's house. Thanks for the offer, though."

"Be careful and keep an eye on her." Kenneth spoke to Eli, then addressed Charlie. "I thought you should know I asked Miss Flanagan if I could court her, and she agreed. If it hadn't been for you and your husband, I never would have met her and recognized what a good woman she is."

Charlie didn't believe in a fort the size of Laramie, he could have missed the lovely, petite brunette, but she was glad he had found someone to court. He was a good man.

"I hope she marries you. I have a feeling she will keep you on your toes." She grinned at him, and he tipped his hat at both of them and rode back to the soldiers.

"We should find a creek and clean up your cheek." Eli pointed at a group of trees on the horizon. "I expect there's probably something—"

A meow sounded from her saddlebag, and she cursed. "You weren't supposed to hear that."

"Is that damn cat in your bag?" He didn't sound mad, but amused.

"I couldn't leave her there. She wouldn't have survived."

"That's not a tragedy."

"I like her and she likes me." She reached back to pet the cat. "I wanted to name her Gaston."

Her father would have laughed to know she'd named a cat after him, but she had been her father's daughter. The sun and the moon rose over him, and when he died, it had devastated her. The cat gave her comfort, and she protected her in her own feline way.

"She doesn't sleep with us. That's my condition for keeping that bag of bones." Eli had given in much quicker than she expected.

"Fine, but cats have their own minds," she teased Eli.

"I would kick her out no matter how sharp her claws." Eli glanced at her cheek. "Let's go take care of that wound and maybe stop for a rest."

She heard the undertone in his voice and happiness bubbled up inside her. Everything would work out and they would be happy. Life had truly begun for their little family.

Chapter Fifteen

Their adventure had been less than what Charlie had wanted, and ended with a disaster followed by a new beginning. Eli was delighted to return back to the fort. His mother would be glad to see them too.

Just when he thought he had Charlie figured out, she changed and he had to start all over again. Not that he would complain. It was why he loved her. She was unique and would always bring life into his world.

Volner had tried to end her life and Eli experienced intense satisfaction when he killed the man. Not because the sergeant had spent his time punching, tripping and torturing Eli at the fort, including taking perverse pleasure in calling him Fixit, but because Volner had dared to hurt Charlie, more than once. The killing of that man had burst the bubble of fury Eli had been choking on. He could take care of his wife no matter what. Of course, she had been grazed by a bullet, and that bothered him. No matter what she said, he would look at that scar and wish he could kill Volner all over again.

They rode toward the tree line to clean her up. She kept dabbing at her cheek and peering at the handkerchief. The graze wasn't bleeding profusely, but he had no doubt it hurt. Perhaps they could rest for a while after doctoring her cheek.

No one was missing them and their lives were an open prairie in front of them. They had nothing standing in their way and no impediments to their future. It was liberating and a bit terrifying.

What did he know about being a husband? He had a ridiculously poor model in his father. Mason had given him advice now and then, and showed Eli what a husband should be. That didn't mean Eli was ready to be all he could for Charlie, but he was damn sure going to try.

As they rode closer to the trees, he heard burbling water. "Sounds like we're in luck. There is water here."

"Good. My cheek stings." She frowned. "I've got a packet Isabelle gave me. She wrote down instructions, which is good because I can never remember what does what."

They dismounted and secured the horses to a branch, then headed for the stream. Charlie sat on a rock with a wrapped packet and handed it to him. "Take this and read what she wrote." She dipped the handkerchief into the water and gently cleaned at the wound, wincing as she did.

"Good thing my father insisted I learn to read the Bible so I can follow my wife's orders now." He grinned when she stuck out her tongue.

Eli untied the twine and unwrapped the package. A few packets of paper were carefully folded inside along with a paper with neat, even writing. He read the instructions and found the one marked yarrow.

"This one is supposed to stop bleeding and help with swelling." He spent the next few minutes cleaning her cheek as best he could, then adding water to the yarrow. "I have to put this on the wound."

"Like hell you will." She held out her hand. "I'll do it. I don't want to have to punch you if you hurt me."

"Fair enough." He held out his hand and she dipped her fingers in the mash, dabbing it on her cheek. "Don't mess up your beautiful face."

She snorted. "You are blind."

He shrugged. "I've heard love is blind, but not in this case. You *are* beautiful."

"I've looked better."

"You've looked worse."

She smacked his shoulder. "You're supposed to flatter me."

"No, I'm not. You'd punch me if I did."

"Yeah I would." She cleaned her fingers off in the water. "Are we really done with all the horrible things?"

He nodded. "It's just you and me, honey. How about I set up a picnic for us?"

"I think I can see my way to picnic with you." She raised one brow. "What did you have in mind?"

He cupped her chin and kissed her. "I thought I would make love to my wife."

"Really? I reckon I would like that." She grinned and made a shooing motion with her hand. "Get busy, husband."

He almost tripped over his big feet running back to the horses for their blankets and the sack of food that was left. He shook with anticipation and need. He wanted to fall on her and lose himself in her body, but he wouldn't.

This was too important to lose control right away. He wanted to savor her and the moment. As he shook out the blanket on the softest grass, he watched her. Just looking at his wife made him hard. Charlie was everything to him, best friend, wife, partner. She owned his heart.

He returned to her side and bowed. "Your bed awaits, my lady."

She tied the packet back up and put it in her saddlebags. With a grin, she managed a curtsey.

"I don't plan on calling you my lord, though."

He laughed and held out his hand. She threaded their fingers together and they walked to the makeshift bed.

"One of these days we're going to do this in a real bed." He turned her toward him and peered at the wound, now covered with a yarrow poultice. "I'm sorry you got hurt."

She shrugged. "It could have been worse. We're both alive and together."

"Partners." He smiled and kissed her. Their mouths fused together and the simple kiss turned into something more. Heat raced through him and he pulled her against him, his hardness and her softness.

"I think we need to get naked." He cupped her breasts and pinched the nipples. She sucked in a breath and cupped his cock through his trousers.

"Yep. Naked. Now."

They stripped the clothes off each other in haste, pulling and yanking until they fell onto the blanket in a tangle of arms and legs. He found a nipple and took it into his mouth, sucking and nibbling at the sweet peak. She moaned and pulled at his shoulders.

"Don't make me wait."

He grinned even as his body pulsed and ached with need to thrust into her. "Anticipation makes it sweeter."

"No, it makes me grumpy." She tugged at his hair. "Now, Eli. Now."

He lapped at the other breast as he sank into the heat between her legs. Heaven could not possibly be any sweeter than this moment. He bit her nipple as he thrust into her.

She groaned and pulled at his hair again. "More."

It seemed both of them liked a little pain with their pleasure. Another reason they were so compatible in every way. He picked up his pace, slamming into her pussy so his pelvis hit her clit each time. She moved with him in perfect rhythm, pulling at his ass to urge him to go faster.

She wrapped her legs around his hips and he drove impossibly deep into her body, into her womb, into her life. His release started in his feet and traveled upwards. He bit her other nipple and she screamed his name, her pussy walls fluttering and tightening around him.

As the pleasure roared through him, he shouted, "I love you," as he spilled his seed deep into her body. There was nowhere and no one he ever wanted as much as he did Charlie.

She was his heart, his life, his soul. She was everything.

The closer they rode to Frankie's house, the tighter Charlie's stomach got. She hadn't seen her eldest sister in more than six months and she'd never gone to her house without Isabelle. Charlie wasn't scared, not really—she was anxious.

The trip from their little glen of happiness had been uneventful, with plentiful game, berries and water for them and the horses. They'd made love every night and every morning, reveling in each other's bodies. She'd learned what he liked and what made him moan. Being alone with him for an entire week had brought them closer than they'd ever been. Charlie couldn't imagine what her life would have been like if she hadn't seen Eli naked. It seemed so long ago.

Seeing Frankie would make everything real. Her eldest sister knew nothing of Charlie's marriage unless Isabelle had written, which was possible.

As they rode up toward the ranch, she marveled at all Frankie and her husband John had built in ten years. A big house, barn, several corrals of the best horseflesh for a hundred miles—and children. They'd been lucky enough to have five boys, Raymond, Ethan, Brett, Trevor and baby Jack. She hadn't met the baby yet, but he was surely as beautiful as his older brothers.

The sound of boys whooping and screeching echoed through the air. Laughter and foolishness in the late afternoon was common at the Malloys'. Someone must have spotted Charlie and Eli because the noise and pack of children headed toward them.

The oldest, Ray, nine and a serious-minded boy, led the way. As they ran across the yard, Trevor stumbled and fell, wailing as he scraped up his hands. Ray stopped and helped him up, brushed off the dirt and must have said something to Trevor to ease the hurt. The smallest of the four, he straightened his shoulders and ran after his brothers with Ray at his side.

"Aunt Charlie!" Ethan and Brett screamed in unison.

Charlie's horse shied a bit from the noise, but she patted his neck and murmured in his ear. "You know these boys. They feed you those oats you love." The gelding seemed to recognize the ranch because he calmed and tossed his head, a sure sign he was happy.

"They're, ah, noisy." Eli watched her nephews with trepidation.

"You have no idea." She laughed and dismounted. The boys surrounded her with squeals of joy, hugs and kisses. She greeted each one and made sure he knew she was glad to see him.

Ray looked at Eli with a scowl. "Who's that man?"

Charlie ruffled her nephew's hair. "That man is my husband, Eli Sylvester."

"You got two first names?" Brett blinked up at Eli.

"I suppose I do." Eli dismounted and stood beside Charlie.

Trevor craned his neck to peer at Eli. The four-year-old had a smear of something orange decorating his cheek. "You're taller than a tree!"

"Maybe. Depends on if the tree is little or not."

Trevor frowned. "I ain't little."

"That's not what I meant. You'll grow big, and, uh." Eli looked at Charlie helplessly.

Charlie took pity on her husband. "Where is your mother?"

"She's in the house, making supper." Brett wiped his nose on his dirty sleeve. "She said don't come in the house 'til she rings the bell."

Charlie smiled. "Maybe you boys can help Eli with the horses and the cat."

Shouts of "Me, me, me!" were almost deafening. She laughed at Eli's expression and kissed him to choruses of "Ewww!" before she headed for the house. It was time to talk to Frankie.

Charlie stepped into the house and the smell of supper cooking washed over her. It reminded her of Maman, being home and feeling safe and loved. She had forgotten how potent the scent of something was. This hit her like a punch to the gut and stole her breath for a moment.

"I told you boys to stay outside. I cannot—" Frankie started to admonish her children, then stopped when she saw Charlie. A smile spread across her face. "Charlotte, *chéri.*"

Just like that Charlie was enfolded in her sister's arms and she once again found herself weeping. Frankie led her to the settee, the one she'd insisted John buy from someplace back east. Fancy for a Wyoming ranch, but perfect for the petite Frankie. The maroon cushions were comfortable and welcoming.

They sat side by side for a few moments while Frankie murmured into her ear, just as Maman used to do when any of them were upset. It was a comfort and just what Charlie needed.

"I do not see you for so long and then you appear crying and wearing a wedding band." Frankie examined Charlie's hand. "It is a lovely ring. I hope there is a man who gave it to you."

"Yes, there is." Charlie laughed and wiped her face with her already dirty hands.

Frankie tutted and gave her a handkerchief from her sleeve. "You will never change, *chéri*."

"No, I've changed. That's why I'm here. I have a story to tell you and Jo. My story." Charlie used the handkerchief to placate her sister. "Do you think Ray can go fetch her?"

Jo lived only half an hour from Frankie with her husband Declan, also a Malloy, although he was born a different man. The west had changed him, as it had everyone.

"*Oui*, of course. Let me call him." Frankie started to rise, but Charlie stopped her.

"My husband is in the barn with the boys." It still felt strange to use the word husband, but she knew now there could be no other man except the one she loved. "His name is Eli Sylvester."

Frankie's brows rose. She had the same sunset-colored hair Charlie had, but without the frizzy cloud. The eldest Chastain also had green eyes, whereas Charlie had hazel. They had similar facial structure, although Charlie seemed to tower over her tiny sister.

"*The* Eli? You married him, then? Isabelle said you loved him but could not see it." Frankie kissed both of Charlie's cheeks, then her forehead, and smiled broadly. "I am so happy for you, *tamia*. I can see in your eyes he is your man and you are his woman, *oui?*"

"Yes, we've been married for a few weeks, and that's another story to tell." Charlie settled into the settee and waited while Frankie went to tell

Ray to head to his aunt's house.

When her sister came back into the house, she was laughing. "The boys are gathered around him as though he was Father Christmas. Your Eli is a lovely man."

Charlie smiled. "Yeah, he is lovely, isn't he?"

"I must stir supper and then we will talk." Frankie went into her kitchen and fussed around with the meal.

Charlie closed her eyes for just a moment, then sleep claimed her.

"*Tamia*, wake up." The lilting voice tickled at Charlie's ear. She was dreaming of making love with Eli near the creek again. Yet the voice kept pulling her up from the very nice dream. "You must wake up."

Her eyelids were so heavy, but she tried to open them anyway. She blinked against the light and focused on the face hovering over hers. Not face, but faces. Lots of faces.

Jo sat beside her, ringed by Frankie holding baby Jack, the other four boys, Frankie's husband John and Eli. Charlie sat up with a jolt. She looked from face to face and saw only happiness and a bit of concern. The cat was curled up beside her, purring and warm. Charlie sat up, displacing the cat with a disgusting meow.

"Jo." She smiled at her bespectacled sister. "I've missed you."

Jo, the only sister with dark brown hair like Papa, pulled her into a hug. As the former governess, she taught her sons and Frankie's sons each day. It was a gaggle of boys who were growing up together, loved and cherished. Jut like Maman and Papa had done for them.

"I missed you too." Jo cupped her face. "You were exhausted. Your Eli asked us to let you sleep. Declan had to stay home with the boys, but I had to come to see you. Levi and Isaac are both sick with a cold."

Eli stood behind everyone, a soft expression on his face. He winked at Charlie. She shook her head at his foolishness.

"It's been a long few weeks since we left Fort Laramie." She rubbed her eyes and then frowned at everyone. "When's supper? I'm starving."

The boys shouted about their own hunger and growling bellies. John picked up Trevor and Brett under his arms.

"It's good to see you, brat." He smiled at Charlie. "Even if these little scamps have no manners." John was a big man with bright blue eyes and wavy brown hair. Handsome, charming and incorrigible. He loved Frankie as much as she loved him.

"You too. Did you meet Eli?" Charlie got to her feet and stretched her kinked muscles.

"I did. The boys can't stop talking about him." John shot Eli an assessing look. "He still has to prove he's worthy of my little sister, though."

Charlie snorted. "Not hardly. You know the only person whose opinion matters is me."

"You are too much like my wife." John walked off with the boys hanging off him like the monkeys they were, squealing and laughing.

"I like your family." Eli kissed her. "I mean, I already liked Isabelle and Mason, but I like these folks too."

"I am going to tell them about what happened to me and how we came to be married." She had to share so she could move on to the rest of her life.

"I'll be right there with you." He took her hand and squeezed. "Does the cat have to come with us?"

She raised one brow. "Of course she does. Her name is Gaston and she's my cat."

"Fine, but she still isn't sleeping in the bed with us. Wherever that bed is." He reached down and scratched the cat behind the ears. With a meow, it moved away, tail in the air. "She still doesn't like me."

Her heart sang from the love in his eyes. She kissed him back. "Well, the cat doesn't need to like you. I love you. I've woken up from a damn long sleep. I'm ready to live."

"Good because I've been waiting a long time to be with you. I love you, Charlie."

She held those words tight, never willing to let them go. "Are you ready for a marriage with a trouser-wearing, cussing, hunter female with a short temper who can't cook?"

"I am. Are you ready for life with a tall, clumsy man who eats more than two people, can fix anything and snores?" He smiled.

"I am."

"Then let's get to it, wife."

She bumped his shoulder. "Damn right, husband."

Laughing, with more love in her heart than she thought possible, Charlie and Eli joined her family for supper. The future was theirs. Together to love and live side by side. A team that was meant to be.

Epilogue

"She's where?" Eli stared at Isabelle, his jaw tight and his gut churning.

"You heard me." Isabelle folded the towel and set it on the shelf in her medical office. "She refused to listen to me and she's stronger and bigger than me, especially now that she's pregnant."

"You should have stopped her." Eli rushed out and ran toward the woods. He ignored Isabelle's response, since she was likely telling him that his wife was a force of nature. He knew that, but now she was out hunting by herself in the woods. And she was almost nine months pregnant.

Her trousers didn't fit anymore so she had taken a dress and cut it in half, sewed the edges to make a unique pair of calico trousers with lace cuffs. She didn't care how she looked or who stared at her, but then again, she never had. Throughout her pregnancy, she'd had strange cravings, rearranged their new cabin three times and cried on a daily basis. She also ate every bit of food she got her hands on. Thank goodness his mother could cook since neither Eli nor Charlie could.

It had been a wonderful, exasperating and thrilling nine months. Now that she was within days of giving birth, she'd decided to go hunting by herself. He would wring her neck when he found her.

He raced into the woods straight for her favorite spot. She couldn't climb trees any longer, but she would no doubt find a way to hunt. He scanned the woods as he went, but there was no sign of her. She would have gone further in, he was sure of it.

A low-pitched moan sounded from ahead. That was Charlie. His heart pounded as he ran toward the sound. He found her in her makeshift trouser dress, covered in blood, leaning against a tree and clutching her belly. Her bow and quiver were in her hand. His heart stopped and he fell to his knees in front of her and touched her distended belly.

"Sweet Jesus, honey, what happened? Is the baby coming? Are you in pain?"

She smacked his hand away. "Yes, the baby is coming and yes I'm in fucking pain!"

"The blood. There's so much of it." The coppery scent filled his nose, making his stomach flip. "Is that normal? We need to get to Isabelle."

He tried to pick her up, but she slapped his hand away again. "That's not my blood." She raised her head and grinned at him. "I got Big Buck."

He stared at her, his heart still pounding so hard, his ribs hurt. "You did what?"

"You heard me. I got Big Buck. Right through the heart. Zing!" She made an arrow motion with her hand. "I had to dress the kill, and that's when my water broke. It goddamn hurts."

Eli swallowed the lump in his throat until he could speak again. "You were dressing a kill in the woods while you were in labor?" He knew he was shouting, but he couldn't seem to stop himself.

"Don't yell at me." She moaned again and tried to squat on the ground. He pulled her back to her feet. "Damn you, Eli."

"We need to get to Isabelle."

"And then come back and get Big Buck. I managed to string him up on the tree using the branch for leverage—"

"Jesus Christ, woman!" He scooped her up in his arms no matter how much she protested. "You have lost your mind."

"Don't jiggle me too much or I'll pee on you," she grumbled in his ear, promising retribution for his high-handedness.

"I don't care if you shit on me. I'm getting you to your sister so you can deliver our baby." He was scared to pieces for her. He had no experience with women in labor, although Isabelle told him Charlie was healthy, as was the baby. He held his entire heart in his arms.

Nothing could happen to Charlie.

Charlie wouldn't admit it to Eli, but she was scared. Quaking in her boots. She wanted to weep and wail like a female, but she didn't. She was strong and tough. Having a baby wasn't that hard. Women did it every day, every minute of every day. She could do it. She would do it.

She was afraid she couldn't do it.

Eli got her to Isabelle's door in record time. Good thing he had long legs. His heart pounded against her side. He was as afraid as she was. It made her feel a little less scared to know she wasn't alone.

"Isabelle!" Eli kicked at the door.

Iz opened the door in a hurry, her eyes wide. She spotted Charlie, who no doubt looked mad with blood everywhere, and her face blanched.

"It's not mine. I got an elk before labor started."

Her sister's color began to return. "You scared me. I'm not a doctor, Charlie, and I don't know what I would do if you needed one."

Eli carried her in and set her on the exam table. "You would do what you've always done. Figure out how to save your patient." He had the same faith in Isabelle that Charlie did.

"I need to wash my hands." Isabelle closed the door. "Get her out of those bloody clothes."

"You want me naked?" Charlie almost screeched.

Isabelle sighed. "You're not wearing anything under that?"

"Well, no, it's hot." Charlie didn't want to explain her undergarments to her sister.

"Eli, go get her nightgown and be quick." Isabelle shooed him out the door. "I'll get everything else ready."

Charlie almost smiled at how fast her husband flew out the door. He was very sweet and she was lucky to have him as her partner. Another pain ripped through her and she gasped.

Isabelle was washing her hands in the deep basin she had beside the small stove. She always kept hot water ready for patients. "How long has it been since the last contraction?"

"I don't know. Ten minutes, maybe fifteen." Charlie gritted her teeth against the pain.

"Did your water break?"

"Yes."

"When?"

"Almost an hour ago! What difference does that make?" Charlie screamed at the height of the contraction, then was able to take a breath as her body loosened.

"An hour? What were you doing all that time when you should have been here?" Isabelle dried her hands with a scowl.

"Doing what I had to do. Keeping a promise I made years ago. Now I can be a mother to my child without regrets." Charlie couldn't explain why she had to take down the buck, but she knew in her gut it had been the right thing. Life would change significantly with a child. Now her past could stay behind her and the future would be in front.

"Later we can discuss how foolish that was. For now we're going to get that baby born healthy." While Isabelle arranged her instruments, the door burst open.

Eli stumbled in, looking more like the boy she remembered meeting one snowy day. He held out the nightgown with a shaking hand. "Here it is."

"Help her change and then we can clean her up." Isabelle was all business when she worked as a healer. A lot less sweet than she normally was. Charlie couldn't take it personally even if she wanted to.

Eli made quick work of taking off her clothes, which he never had trouble doing, and Isabelle washed her before putting on her nightgown. Isabelle put a towel under Charlie and then glanced at Eli.

"I have to examine her."

Eli looked completely horrified. "All right."

"Go get Big Buck and bring it back to the smoking shed." Charlie wasn't going to lose the meat, rack or pelt. That big animal would provide a great deal of money she might need for the baby.

"What? I'm not going anywhere."

"Yes, you are. Go get that goddamn elk or I'll never forgive you." Charlie shook her fist at him. "I might even punch you in the balls."

Isabelle laughed while Eli took a step backward.

"How long will it be?" Eli asked Isabelle.

"I don't know and neither does the baby. At least a few hours." Isabelle patted his shoulder. "Do what she asks."

"What she told me to do." He frowned.

"Go get the elk or she won't stop nagging you." Isabelle opened the door. "I promise she won't have the baby until you return."

Eli stood at Charlie's side and spread his large palm on her belly. "I love you."

It was all he needed to say and all she needed to hear. She managed a crooked smile. "I love you too. Now get moving so you can come back. I want to have this baby."

He kissed her hard, then kissed her belly and flew out the door. Charlie's eyes pricked with tears.

"He is a wonderful man and he's going to be a wonderful father." Isabelle took Charlie's hand. "Do you want him here for the birth? Mason had been exposed to birth on the plantation he grew up on, and the process was familiar, if frightening. Eli has nothing to draw from."

Charlie had little time to consider whether Eli would stay after he returned. The business of birthing a baby was messy, painful and the most exhausting experience of her life. Time passed and the two of them worked in tandem. As the contractions grew closer together, Isabelle mopped her brow.

"You're doing well. The labor is progressing more quickly than I expected. Your son or daughter is anxious to greet the world." Isabelle checked inside Charlie once more. "I believe you're ready to push, *tamia*."

Charlie wiped the sweaty hair off her cheek. "Eli isn't back yet. You promised him."

"Babies do not wait for their fathers if they have a mind to make their entrance. I will apologize to him." Isabelle fetched a clean towel from the stack on the shelf and positioned herself between Charlie's legs. "When the contraction begins, push. Do you understand?"

Charlie had never worked so hard in her life. She screamed, grunted, cursed, pulled a piece of the table off with her bare hands—and most of all, she pushed. Her child depended on her to do her best, and she was not about to let that baby down.

"The head is crowning. One more big one." Isabelle looked awful with her hair hanging in strands around her perspiring face. Her expression was of determination and focus.

"Thank you, Iz." Charlie didn't want to forget to say it. "Thank you for helping and for being here for me."

"Always." Iz patted Charlie's foot. "Now, let's get this baby born. Ready?"

Charlie pushed with every fiber of her being and the baby slid out into Isabelle's waiting hands. The door burst open and Eli stood there, his dark hair a mass of windblown knots, his eyes uncertain. He saw the baby and paled.

"I missed it."

"No, you're here for the best part." Isabelle made quick work of cleaning the baby, cutting the cord and swaddling it in the blanket.

Charlie was exhausted beyond measure, but she watched as her sister handed Eli the tiny bundle with a smile in her heart. This was what life was all about. Being loved and loving in return. Sharing ups and downs, triumphs and tragedies. Eli was her partner, always at her side.

"I'd like you to meet your daughter." Isabelle beamed at Charlie. "It's a girl."

Eli gazed down at the baby and walked over to Charlie. He kissed the baby's forehead and laid her in Charlie's arms. "She's the most beautiful thing I've ever seen."

Charlie never expected to be a mother, never wanting to be one, but at that moment, she wondered how in the hell she had ever thought that. The baby was a perfect angel, with Eli's dark hair and Charlie's short nose.

"Hello, Marie." She kissed the baby's soft forehead. "Welcome to our family."

Eli smiled at the two of them. "I love you both so much, my heart is about to burst."

"Don't do that, because I need you. *She* needs you." Charlie took his hand. "I love you too."

The last Chastain sister had finally found what she sought. Her happiness was found in the wilds of Wyoming, beside a man who loved her for who she was, not the color of her hair or the clothes she wore.

Life had come full circle and they had created a child of their own. Love had triumphed over all.

About the Author

Beth Williamson, who also writes as Emma Lang, is an award-winning, bestselling author of both historical and contemporary romances. Her books range from sensual to scorching hot. She is a Career Achievement Award Nominee in Erotic Romance by Romantic Times Magazine, in both 2009 and 2010.

Beth has always been a dreamer, never able to escape her imagination. It led her to the craft of writing romance novels. She's passionate about purple, books and her family. She has a weakness for shoes and purses, as well as bookstores. Her path in life has taken several right turns, but she's been with the man of her dreams for more than twenty years.

Beth works full-time and writes romance novels evenings, weekends, early mornings and whenever there is a break in the madness. She is compassionate, funny, a bit reserved at times, tenacious and a little quirky. Her cowboys and Western romances speak of a bygone era, bringing her readers to an age where men were honest, hard and packing heat. For a change of pace, she also dives into some smokin' hot contemporaries, bringing you heat, romance and snappy dialogue.

Life might be chaotic, as life usually is, but Beth always keeps a smile on her face, a song in her heart, and a cowboy on her mind. ;)

www.bethwilliamson.com

When life falls apart, love can make you whole again.

The Jewel
© *2014 Beth Williamson*

The Malloy Family, Book 11

As the "beautiful" sister, Isabelle Chastain always struggled to be taken seriously. But as her family immigrates to Oregon Territory, she loses her sister Francesca to marriage, and her parents to dysentery. It's time to take control.

With an empty wagon and a broken heart, she and her younger sister Charlotte turn for home to search for another sister, Josephine, left behind to recover from typhoid. The last thing Isabelle needs in her path is a naked, bleeding man left to die in the dirt.

Dazzled by a friend's stories of California gold, college professor Mason Bennett left North Carolina to get his share. All his dreams of adventure and riches got him, however, was robbed, beaten, and left for dead.

As Isabelle stitches him up, he discovers her wit is as sharp as her needle. But when vagabonds seize their wagon, they must band together to save themselves—or any hope for a happy future could disappear.

Warning: Saddle up for an Old West yarn, complete with a beautiful woman with more strength than ten men, a professor turned cowboy, a love that defies the odds, and adventure that will leave you gasping for more.

Running from the past…and running out of time.

The Fortune
© *2013 Beth Williamson*

The Malloy Family, Book 9

French-born Francesca Chastain came to New York with her family to find a better life. Now she is fleeing a nightmare. Her past chases her from New York and she must run, and run hard.

Her journey to the land of milk and honey is interrupted by the accidental squeeze of a trigger. And the man on the other end of her blunder is a man like none other she's ever met.

After three years working Oregon-bound wagon trains, John Malloy has almost saved enough money to start his own horse ranch. And almost met the end of his life at the hands of fiery, green-eyed Frankie, a confusing, frustrating woman who responds to his flirting—then disappears.

No one is more relieved than Frankie when John races to her rescue, but now they're trapped in the wild. And the shadows of both their pasts are closing in…

Warning: Inside you'll find sexy heat, danger, Old West violence, gun-toting bad guys and an emotional roller coaster. Prepare to fall in love with the Malloys all over again with witty, strong women, stubborn, heroic men and a love that launched a legacy.

The lie that saves her life could destroy their love.

The Prospect
© *2014 Beth Williamson*

The Malloy Family, Book 10

Josephine Chastain never thought a case of typhoid would force her Oregon-bound family to leave her behind in Fort John—in the care of the last man she trusts. Others in the wagon train may have accepted Declan Calhoun's motives for kidnapping her sister Frankie, but not Jo.

When she wakes up from the three-week fever, though, she finds some things have changed. Declan is her husband. And their cabin is too small to contain the growing desire between them.

While Jo fights for her life, Declan finds himself falling for the bookish Chastain sister. A woman with a spine of steel and a seemingly bottomless well of smarts. In other words, everything he can never be.

Yet now is not the time to confess the little white lie that has thus far kept her safe. Not when he must figure out how to escape a quarantine that's turned into extortion. And resist Jo's determination to seduce him before she learns the truth. Before the unforgiving wilderness between them and safety claims their lives.

Warning: Be ready for a learned but stubborn woman, a man with a dark past who needs redeeming, and an adventure that will light your hair and your panties on fire.

It's all about the story...

Romance

HORROR

www.samhainpublishing.com